BABY GIRL

BABY GIRL

Sami King-Wente

Pen & Ivy Press
Turlock, California

Library of Congress Number:		98-87149
ISBN#:	(Hard Cover)	0-7388-0079-1
	(Soft Cover)	0-7388-0080-5

This book was printed in the United States of America.

To order additional copies of this book, contact:
Xlibris Corporation
1-888-7-XLIBRIS
www.Xlibris.com

ACKNOWLEDGEMENTS

I thank then-Lieutenant Lonald Lott of the Turlock Police Department for his invaluable insight into the inner workings of a detective squad. His information allowed me to take literary license with some legal procedures. I thank the body of Christ that is Turlock Community Fellowship for their prayers and support through false starts and disappointments. I thank my family - immediate and extended - for always believing I had the talent and the drive to make this happen. And, a special thank you to Brian who has worked tirelessly on behalf of myself and my book; I love you, Angel!

FOR DOUG

Monday, October 31

"Trick or treat!"

Four costumed candy-seekers stood on Jersey Masters' doorstep, offering up their bags. The sky wore dusk. San Diego's Indian summer clutched at the remnants of the day.

"Don't you all look great!" She exclaimed. "Okay, I've got peanut butter cups and chocolate mint patties. What's your pleasure?"

A little cowgirl stepped forward. "P'nut butter cup, please."

"Me, too." An astronaut thrust his bag at her.

Jersey dropped an orange square into each bag. A tiny fairy toddled around the bigger children, clutching a weighted pillowcase.

"Peanut butter cup?"

The little girl nodded and watched it slide down the side of her bag. A ten-year-old Madonna waited her turn then took a peppermint patty.

"Thanks," she called, and ran after the others.

"What kind of mother sends her daughter out in a bra made of foil-covered snow cone cups?" She wondered, aloud. Jersey carried her crystal bowl of treats into the living room.

"Can I have a peanut butter one, too?"

Jersey looked down at her little girl, kneeling in front of a coloring book on the coffee table. Golden curls and wide green eyes made the child a miniature version of herself. Her rosebud mouth was streaked with chocolate.

"You've already had three, Jenna. Aren't you getting a little queasy?"

"My tummy doesn't hurt, honest. Could I have only one more?"

"All right, Honey Bunny. You 'could have only one more'."

"Okay!" Jenna tore off the wrapper.

The doorbell chimed, again. Jersey picked up the goodies and headed into the foyer. Behind her, Jenna smacked satisfactorily. She balanced the bowl on her hip with one hand and opened the door with the other, ready to exclaim over the children's costumes. Instead, she encountered a pair of khaki trousers. She looked up into the gray-green eyes of a man in his late fifties. Gray salted his dark hair; steel-rimmed glasses diminished his eyes. A chill ran down her spine.

"Excuse me," Jersey said. "I thought you were trick-or-treaters."

"I'm looking for Miss Jersey Masters," he said.

"I'm Jersey Master." Her stomach crawled with apprehension. Jenna peeked around her.

"Jenna! It's Daddy."

Jenna's little fingers clamped down hard on Jersey's thigh.

"What do you want?" Jersey snapped.

He stepped across the threshold. Her insides shrank back. The bowl crashed to the floor. Glass and candy flew in all directions. His black, heavy shoes clunked on the tile floor. Jenna cringed at the sound. Involuntarily, Jersey stepped back.

"I've been trying to reach you for weeks, Jenna. Why haven't you returned any of my calls or letters?"

He moved in. Jersey swallowed hard. Her apprehension congealed into anger. Her mouth came down as her chin went up.

"We have nothing to say to each other. Please, leave."

He frowned. "I don't understand."

"Certainly, you do not. I want you to leave." Jersey grabbed the doorknob for emphasis. Behind her, Jenna looked at him with one eye. Jersey felt her shudder.

"Baby Girl?" His eyes appealed to the child.

Jersey leapt onto the landing. Jenna clung to her and began to cry. Jersey lifted the child into her arms. Her own hands trembled, making her furious.

"Get out of my house!" She spat.

"Jenna, please —"

"You're not appealing to a child any longer, you must deal with a woman now. I warn you, I have a gun upstairs. If you refuse to leave, I will use it."

Jersey backed away. He followed as far as the landing and grasped the black iron newel post.

"I only want to talk to you, Baby Girl. Please, can't we just sit down and —"

"No! Get out of my house."

Jersey ran up the stairs, Jenna crying and clinging to her. In her bedroom, Jersey flipped on the lights and set the child on the floor.

"Is he gonna get us?" Jenna sobbed.

"No, he isn't, Honey Bunny. Not while I have anything to say about it. You just stay put, okay?"

Jersey scrambled across her bed and yanked open the drawer of her night chest. There lay the gun; it gleamed in the golden lamplight. She snatched it up, undoing the safety clasp as she hurried back to the door. Jenna stood rooted where Jersey had put her. His footsteps thumped on the stairs. They both froze. Jenna's green eyes widened.

"Jenna?" He called.

"No, no, nonono!" Jenna screamed and ran for the closet.

Jersey slipped into the doorway. He was headed for Jenna's bedroom. She aimed the gun at him.

"Stop right there."

He wheeled around at the sound of her voice. He saw the silver barrel pointed at his chest. His face drained of color.

"What are you doing? You aren't serious about using that?"

"I am serious. I want you out of my house, one way or another."

He raised his hands, palms out. "Please. Talk to me. That's all I'm asking. Just talk to me."

Jersey steadied the gun with both hands.

"Baby Girl, please!"

He stepped toward her one, twice. The gun trembled in her fingers. BANG! Bang, bang. He stared at her in disbelief. Jersey stared back. His blood grew on his shirt in three red flowers. He fell forward, his head thudding on the floor. He didn't move. Slowly, silently, still pointing the gun at him, Jersey stepped down. In the middle of the stairs, she stopped and sank to the step behind her. After some time, Jenna tiptoed down the stairs and wrapped herself around Jersey.

"Is he dead, really?" The child whispered.

"Yes, I think so, Jenna. He's really dead."

The child began to shake. "Are we in trouble, now?"

"I don't know, Honey Bunny. I don't know."

Jersey tucked the child under her chin. She rocked the child gently. Blue and red lights splashed over the walls of the foyer. A squad car pulled into her driveway, then another. An ambulance, then a plain brown sedan parked at her curb. Suddenly, her lawn was alive with people.

"The p'liceman's are comin' now, aren't they?"

"Yes."

"Will they make you be in jail?"

"I don't know, Jenna. They might. Your daddy is dead, and I shot him."

"But, he was a bad daddy! He hurted me."

"I know, Honey Bunny. That may not make any difference." Jersey kissed the child, tenderly.

"I will tell them! I'll tell them he was bad. He hurted me and he did come here for me again and I didn't want him to. I didn't want him to!" Jenna began to cry, again.

"Hush, now. Don't worry. You let me tell the police what they need to know."

Quickly, she hid Jenna from sight.

Monday, October 31

Spots of blue, then red stained the white clay walls of 418 Presidio Crest Drive. People in various uniforms traipsed through the cinnamon ferns and lily-of-the-valley that bordered the lawn. Paramedics and EMT's unloaded medical supplies and a gurney. Uniformed officers with guns drawn prepared for anything. Hercules and Pocahontas skirted the lawn, devouring the scene with curious eyes. Detective Spencer Phillips emerged from his sedan. Detective Mateo Rivera strode across the grass to meet him.

"Hey, Spence. How was your niece's recital?" Mateo asked.

"It went great. Too bad you missed it."

"Oh, yeah. That's exactly how I wanted to spend my Saturday night, listening to five- and six-year-olds squeaking out 'Three Blind Mice' on the violin."

"Alison's well beyond the squeaking stage. She's all the way up to screaming cat. So, what's going on here, Rivera?"

"Don't know yet. Everyone's just arriving, so the crime scene's fresh. 911 got a call about twenty minutes ago. Little girl said she shot her dad."

"Kids and guns." Phillips shook his head in disgust. "When are we grownups going to learn?"

He focused on the two-story house. Through the open front door, he saw a woman huddled on the stairway, her face a pale triangle framed by chestnut curls. She appeared to be watching the activity on her front lawn.

"Who's the woman? The mother?"

Mateo shrugged. "Haven't asked yet."

"Is this how you found things?" Phillips indicated the open door. "No one's been inside?"

Rivera shook his head no.

"Any witnesses?"

"None that we've determined. Of course, any trick-or-treaters are home counting their goodies. I'll start the uniforms canvassing the area."

"Apparently, her neighbors are not the curious type." Phillips said, observing the empty sidewalk.

The detectives approached the house, each surveying the surroundings. Phillips was in his mid thirties; six feet, three inches tall, red-gold hair. He wore a brown serge suit, white shirt and narrow brown tie. His Latino partner was ten years younger and several inches shorter. His jet-black hair was fashionably cut, as was his suit; a pair of designer sunglasses dangled from his jacket pocket. The woman rose as they approached and wiped her palms down her jeaned legs. She walked down the stairs and waited in the doorway. Phillips produced a badge and held it out for her inspection.

"Good evening, ma'am. I'm Detective Phillips with the San Diego homicide division. This is my partner, Detective Rivera. Did you report a shooting?"

Phillips noted her appearance in a single glance. Slender and delicately boned, she wore a white Oxford button-down tucked into faded blue denims. Bare feet. Her hair was disheveled and tears clung to her lashes. Her eyes were green; they had appraised him, as well. Now, their eyes met.

"Come in, gentlemen." Her voice was calm, warm. "The body is at the top of the stairs. I'm sure he is dead. He hasn't moved or made a sound in some time."

Two officers followed and began to dust for fingerprints, while a photographer gathered pictorial evidence. Rivera instructed them to include the entire front entry into the kitchen, as well as the upstairs. He then directed the paramedics to the body. Rivera had been a detective for two years, an officer for ten. Growing up in the barrios of Chula Vista, Mateo had watched first his Papa, then his older brother, then his best friend, be gunned down in drive-by shootings. For three years, his Mama wept and prayed, fingering her rosary incessantly, for the street violence to end and leave her one son alive. Once on the force, Mateo worked hard, achieving the rank of detective in record time.

Detective Phillips felt no qualms about turning the investigation over to him. He now turned his attention on the woman. He entered the foyer, cautious not to contaminate any trace evidence. Something crunched under his toe. He looked down. Broken glass and candy were scattered over the brick-colored Mexican tiles.

"I dropped it," she said, wiping her hands on her back pockets.

"I need to ask you some questions." He took a notepad from his jacket. "Would you prefer to have someone with you? A neighbor, a lawyer, perhaps?"

"Do I need a lawyer, Detective?"

"You might feel more comfortable with one present."

"No, I wouldn't. But, I'll answer any questions I can. The ones I can't answer, I won't. Come into the living room."

She led him through an archway to their right and down two steps into the living room. The room was a long rectangle, he observed. A formal dining room was set up in the back half. Through glass-paned French doors, he saw a patio lit with silver moonlight. A second archway on the long inner wall led into her kitchen. The living area was in the front half of the room. Twin cream-colored linen sofas flanked a brick and stucco fireplace. A small table and chairs, swathed in mauve, fronted three large windows that were genuine panes, he noted, unlike the current fad of plastic tubing sandwiched between slices of energy-efficient glass.

Phillips felt uneasy as he settled himself on one of the pale sofas. He felt as if he had stepped into the pages of San Diego Lifestyles magazine. She picked up a coloring book and crayons from the table, stashing them in a blonde armoire. She opened its doors on a well-stocked bar. She tried not to watch the paramedics wheeling away the draped body. She poured herself a brandy. She didn't offer him anything.

"I don't advise you drink that before we complete our interview," he said. "Your statement will be useless."

She rolled her glass in her hands. "Then, let's get started, shall we?"

"Certainly. Name?"

"Jersey Rae, that's R-A-E, Masters."

"Jersey?"

"Like the state, yes. You spell it the same."

"Your occupation, Miss Masters? Is it Miss?"

"Yes. I do public relations. I work from home."

Phillips recorded her answers in his notebook. "Tell me what happened."

"He rang the bell. I normally keep my front door locked, but I thought it was trick-or-treaters. I opened the door. He came at me. I ordered him out, but he wouldn't leave. I warned him I had a gun upstairs. When he still refused to leave, I ran up and got it. I didn't intend to shoot him, only to threaten him into leaving. But, when I came out of my bedroom, he was standing right there. He came at me again, and...I...just fired."

"How many times did you fire the gun?"

"Three, I think," Jersey said.

"Here's the gun, Spence." Rivera handed him a paper bag. "And, this is the guy's identification. One Daniel Miller, age fifty-six. Nevada Driver's license. He's dead, all right. Three entry wounds, one to the heart, no exits. We're about through upstairs. I'll notify Nevada police, in case he had family."

Phillips nodded and handed back the gun. So far, he thought, the shooting came off as self-defense. He turned back to Jersey.

"We'll need your paper work for this," he said to her. "Now, you said Miller rang the bell, you opened the door. He came in, uninvited and you asked him to leave. He refused. At that point, you went upstairs and retrieved your gun from your bedroom. Correct?"

"Yes."

"Which bedroom is yours?"

"The first door at the top of the stairs," Jersey said.

"Where do you normally keep your gun?"

"In a drawer in my night chest, where it was tonight."

"How long have you had it?"

"A couple of years."

He wrote while he talked. "Have you ever fired it before tonight?"

"Just during my lessons. Not since."

"Why didn't you call the police from your bedroom?"

Jersey sighed. "I simply didn't think to."

"When you came out of your bedroom, where was Miller?"

"Halfway down the hall, walking toward Jenna's room."

"And, that's when you shot him?"

"Yes-no. He came at me. His hands were out, to grab me, I thought." Jersey shrugged. "That's when I shot him."

"Three times?"

"I think so, yes."

Phillips sat forward. "Did he say anything to you? Give you any indication why he was here?"

Jersey stared into her glass and shook her head no.

Phillips shifted. "How soon after you shot him did your daughter call 911?" He asked.

Her curtain of lashes flew up. "My daughter?"

"My initial report says a young girl phoned 911 saying she had killed her father. Was that your daughter?"

Jersey inclined her head. "Jenna is my child."

"And, Miller was her father?"

She set her glass on the bar shelf, turning away from him. Spencer studied her body language.

"Yes," she said, at last. "Daniel Miller was Jenna's father."

"How long has it been since you last saw him?"

"I had hoped I would never see him again," she said.

"How long has it actually been?"

"Jenna was five when he left."

"How old is she now?" He pressed.

"Jenna is six. And, I hope your people didn't disturb her room. This evening has been very upsetting for her. I'd like to keep her trauma to a minimum, if possible."

"My niece is six," he said, genially. "I understand your concern."

His attempt at congeniality grated on her like a spoon in a garbage disposal. Jersey threw him a scorching look. Phillips crossed to her side. The top of her head was even with his shoulder. He wanted to read her face, to see what else she was leaving unsaid.

"What was your relationship with Miller? Were you married, or just lovers?"

She met his gaze. His eyes were blue; her look was hard. She ran her gaze down the length of him, studied his shoes, then returned to his face. Spencer felt dissected.

"We were intimate, at one time," she said, bitterly. "We were never lovers."

"He made promises he couldn't keep, huh? Was he already married?"

"Yes, he was."

Phillips set his notepad beside her glass. His voice chilled. "Tell me again what happened, tonight. Why was Miller here? Did he actually threaten you, or your daughter?"

"Leave Jenna out of this. She didn't kill him, I did."

"Where is your daughter now, Miss Masters? How much of what happened did she see?"

Jersey recoiled. "I'm very tired. I would like you to leave."

Phillips grabbed her arm, brought his face down to hers. "You're going to jail, lady," he growled. "Do you understand? I'm a cop. A man is dead, and you admit killing him. You're going to jail unless you start cooperating with me."

Her look challenged him, but she said nothing. Phillips sighed.

"Let's try it another way," he said. "I'll tell you what I'm wondering, you'll tell me how close I am to the truth. Or, we'll go downtown and you will be booked for murder."

Jersey shrugged and still said nothing.

"See, I'm wondering if this is a custody thing. You abducted Miller's child and he tracked you down. Then, you shot him to keep him from taking her back. How'm I doing?"

"I wasn't keeping his child from him, he abandoned her. Daniel Miller was a loathsome bastard."

He flipped open his notepad. "Tell me, again, what happened here. Start at the beginning - the very beginning - and don't leave out anything."

"Tomorrow, please." She said, stifling a yawn. "I'm too tired. I can't think anymore."

"Tonight. I don't want you to think, I want you to talk."

Jersey thrust her wrists at him. "Take me in, Detective. It's obvious you are not interested in what happened. That man came into my home, uninvited. I didn't ask him here, I didn't encourage him to stay. Jenna was terrified, but none of that matters. You're a cop. Your heart is something you hang your badge over."

Spencer deflated. "It is very late," he conceded. "Justice won't be served by dragging a little girl out of her bed. I imagine she's had a really rough night."

"You imagine correctly," Jersey said, coldly.

He pocketed his notebook and tipped an imaginary hat. "Tomorrow. But, I'm posting an officer outside, tonight. He'll discourage any late-night traveling. I'll be here first thing in the morning. And, I'll want to meet your daughter."

Monday, October 31

Jersey followed him to the door, locking it after him. She watched until he drove away, then went into the kitchen for a broom and dustpan. As she swept up the broken glass and ruined candy, Jersey replayed the evening. When had Jenna called the police, she wondered. She remembered nothing after firing the gun. Nothing until the little girl wrapped her arms around her. Jersey thought, I must have been in shock.

She carried the debris back into the kitchen. Jenna must have been terrified, she thought, watching the shards slide into the garbage pail. She put back the equipment, closed the cupboards. At last, she turned out the lights and climbed the stairs. She trailed her hand along the iron banister. Fine, black grit clung to her fingers. Jersey grimaced. Leftovers from the police "dusting," she thought. San Diego's finest spent less than three hours gathering evidence, then left their handiwork for her to clean up. Obviously, the police academy did not teach a course in etiquette. Jersey yawned. She was exhausted, but would she be able to sleep?

"Ugh!" She exclaimed. Blood. Her insides roiled at the sight. Yet, she stared, unable to turn away. The puddle's edges looked dry, crusted, while the middle seeped deeper into the padding.

"I'd better deal with it first thing in the morning," she murmured. "Before Jenna wakes up."

She tiptoed into the little girl's bedroom. Jersey smiled. She loved this room. It was her favorite, large and sunny all day long. She had delighted in turning it into a fairyland. She had decorated with cotton candy pink wallpaper, and cabbage roses on the curtains and bed covers.

She pushed little chairs into a child-sized table. She straightened a shelf of games, then crossed to the bed. Jenna slept fitfully. Small wonder, Jersey thought. She tucked Jenna's little legs beneath the blankets. Her pillow felt damp to the touch. Jenna rolled over, whimpering softly. Jersey soothed the little girl until her brow relaxed and her breathing steadied.

"Sweet dreams, Honey Bunny." Jersey whispered, kissing her forehead. "You don't have to be afraid any more."

She kissed Jenna's heart-shaped mouth. Then, she passed through the adjoining bathroom, through her walk-in closet, getting ready for bed as she went. Her room was as sophisticated as an Egyptian palace with black lacquer furniture and tawny gold fabrics, sumptuous pillows and stoneware lamps.

Jersey climbed into bed and switched off the bedside lamp. She settled back into her pillows and closed her eyes. He was gone; she sighed. Jenna was finally safe. Relief shivered through her. The alarm clock ticked softly. Pale moonlight seeped through lace curtains, mottling the walls and hushing her thoughts. Sleep stole over her at last.

She woke suddenly, surrounded by darkness. The moon had been obliterated; the darkness was everywhere. But, it felt peaceful, almost serene. She gave herself over to the inky blackness. Slowly, she became aware of a presence. Someone - something - waited close by. Jersey sensed it watching her, waiting...for what?

"Who's there?" She called.

But, no one answered. The something reached out to her, urging her to reach back. Her stomach curled in fear.

"Who are you?" She called, again. Again, it didn't answer. Instead, it moved away. Desperation seized her. "Don't go! Who are you?"

She had to follow; she could do nothing else. Loneliness swamped her. The murkiness antagonized her. "Who are you? Please! Don't leave me."

Jersey started out of her pillows, her heart pounding in her throat. A dream! A nightmare, she realized. She let out her terror on a nervous laugh. She was home, in her own bed. Thank God!

She hugged her blanketed knees, leaning her cheek against their creamy softness. Thank God. She breathed easier. Beside her, the clock's ticking reassured her. Its gentle sound comforted her more than any sound she had ever heard. Jersey knew she wouldn't sleep any more tonight.

She tiptoed back into Jenna's room and lay herself next to the sleeping child, wrapping her in her arms. Jenna curled into her side, sighing contentedly. Jersey cradled Jenna, lightly stroking the child's flannel-soft forearm, brushing away any ghosts that dared to flit across her brow. Jenna smelled as fresh and warm as a summer meadow. Hours later, Jersey watched the sun tease the edges of Jenna's window shades.

Tuesday, November 1

"I don't get it," Rivera said. "How does a woman and her little girl live in a neighborhood and not know anyone?"

"It's the Nineties, Mateo. Everyone minds their own business."

Detectives Phillips and Rivera had canvassed the neighborhood for almost an hour. Presidio Crest Drive replicated a Mexican esplanade. Spanish olive trees shaded the sidewalks. Red poured walkways led to white stucco homes trimmed with brick and red roof tiles. A quiet neighborhood for a weekday, Phillips observed. People retrieved their morning newspaper; a middle-aged couple walked their poodle. Once in a while, a car drove away, bound for another day. Phillips rang the doorbell of the next house and looked at his partner, nattily dressed in a straw-colored suit of raw silk. He was wearing his navy-blue worsted jacket over khaki slacks.

"Eight houses and nothing," he said. "No one knows anything about Jersey Masters, or her little girl."

"Man, I don't know why you let the lady off in the first place." Rivera said, his black eyes snapping. "Why are you buying her story? What are you thinking about this woman?"

"From where I stand, the shooting looks justifiable. If otherwise, I want Ms. Masters to have all the rope she needs. Besides, I couldn't drag her little girl out in the middle of the night."

"What little girl? Nobody even saw the kid last night. Spence, for all you know she could be dead, too."

"She wasn't when she called 911. I'll make sure she isn't when

I talk to her mom, this morning."

"Is Jersey Masters hiding her kid? Or, is she just an overprotective mother?"

Phillips chuckled. A small elderly woman cracked the front door, wearing a green chenille bathrobe, eyeing her visitors. Phillips showed his badge and apologized for the early hour. He introduced himself and his partner, then explained for the ninth time their business in the neighborhood. And, for the ninth time was told she didn't know Miss Jersey Masters, or her little girl.

The detectives exchanged glances; same story as before. Phillips handed her a business card, asked her to phone if she could help in any way, and thanked her for her time. The two detectives returned to the sidewalk. What did he think of Jersey Masters, Spencer wondered? She was exasperating, certainly, but did that make her a killer? He knew no one was incapable of murder given the right circumstances. Only a fool would underestimate her. He was no fool.

Rivera rang the next doorbell. A pretty brunette in lavender peddle-pushers answered, a baby riding her hip. Inside, Mr. Rogers invited her preschooler to be his neighbor. Once more, the detectives asked about Jersey Masters and her daughter. Once more, they learned this neighbor had only a nodding acquaintance with the former and had never seen the latter.

"Your kids don't play together?" River asked.

The woman shook her head. "We love her Christmas decorations, though," she volunteered. "My kids are already talking about them."

They headed back to the street. Rivera folded his black overcoat over his arm. "Listen, Spence," he said. "I'd love to continue canvassing neighbors who mind their own business, but I'm due in court."

"All right. I have some unfinished business with Miss Masters, anyway. We'll let the uniforms finish up here. Don't forget, we'll have the 911 tape after lunch."

* * * * * *

Jersey carried her coffee mug into her study. She needed to work, to close her mind to the disturbing images that had chased her through the night. The San Diego Union-Tribune had written a small article on the shooting. It had also been a blurb on the a.m. info-news shows. No reporters were beating down her door, however. Thank goodness.

Her study reflected the true Jersey Masters, she thought. Cherry wood furnishings, classic and timeless in design, and soft cotton fabrics, in muted shades of green, made working even more pleasurable. The long, narrow room afforded space for all her office equipment and a comfortable sitting area for meeting clients. The angle of her desk took advantage of the four large corner windows, shuttered against the morning sun.

She tucked one foot beneath her as she sat down at her desk. The scent of rose potpourri wafted from a silver bowl. Jersey set her mug on a coaster and booted up her computer. Little Mac's cheery smile greeted her. She entered her password, then opened a Christmas layout for a local department store ad. She pasted elves into one display, a candy cane border around another. She sat back, studying the results. The bell chimed in the foyer. Jersey took her coffee to the front door.

"Detective Phillips," she said. He had his notebook in hand, she saw.

"Miss Masters." She wore a periwinkle silk kimono. She had done her makeup and hair. "We need to review your statement, before I turn things over to the district attorney."

"I'm sure you are following standard procedures, detective." She said, crisply. "Won't you please come in."

"If I were following standard procedures, I would have arrested you last night. I took pity on you, for the sake of your daughter."

He stepped inside. Jersey closed and bolted the door. Upstairs, a cleaning service was steam-vacuuming Daniel Miller's blood out of the cinnamon-colored carpet.

"Coffee?" She held up her cup.

"Yes, thank you."

"It won't render my statement useless?"

He returned a wry look. Jersey led him into her kitchen. He seated himself at the dining table, observing his surroundings. The brick-red tiles ran in from the hall. Straw seats cushioned the chairs, serape-print curtains fluttered at the windows. The inviting aroma of Mexican coffee hung in the air. This room too, was immaculate, he thought. No dirty dishes, toys or mess anywhere. He remembered her spotless living room last night.

"Amazing," he muttered. Jersey tossed a quizzical look over her shoulder. "Your house is so neat," he said. "My sister has two kids and her house is a wreck. No one would ever guess a child lives here."

A workman appeared in the doorway. "We're through, upstairs, Miss Masters."

"Thank you."

Spencer waited while she let them out. When she returned, Jersey set a cup in front of him, along with a sugar bowl and creamer, which he ignored. She slid out another chair and lay a Raggedy Ann doll on the table before sitting.

"Jenna puts her things away," she said, coolly.

She folded her hands around her cup and leaned on her elbows. Her nails were short and blunt cut, glossy pink but not polished. She looked directly into his eyes, indicating he could begin. Phillips sipped his coffee and opened his notebook.

"Let's start with your relationship with Daniel Miller."

"Specifically, what would you like to know?" She asked.

"How long you knew each other?"

"Years," she said.

"How long were you intimate?"

"Years."

"Why did you stop seeing each other?"

"He left."

Phillips cupped his face in his hands, sighing. "I appreciate your brevity, Miss Masters," he said. "But, please be a little more forthcoming."

She nodded. Her eyes reminded him of emeralds set in ivory, he thought. He watched her watching him, then shook his head. She was composed; she was intelligent. She would not be forthcoming, he knew.

"Did Miller tell you why he left?"

She shook her head no, shrugging a shoulder. "Things didn't work out?"

"How long into your relationship was Jenna conceived?"

"Right away."

"How did he feel about having a child?"

She grunted in disgust. "He loved her to death, detective."

"Last night, you said you hadn't seen or heard from Miller in a year, correct?"

Jersey broke eye contact, staring into her cup. "Yes," she said.

He noted the lie. She rose from the table and went to stand at the back door, looking out through the bare panes. She folded her arms across her chest, like a shield. Phillips shifted in his chair, studying her. She moved like an abused woman. He had seen too many; though she could be a very good actress, he told himself.

"Was Miller physically abusive to you, Miss Masters?"

She shrank into her robe. Spencer noticed. He didn't need an answer. He knew the look.

"To your child, as well?" He asked, gently.

"Not when I could keep him from her." Her voice faltered. "He took her before I could stop him."

His heart squeezed, painfully. He knew the euphemism well. Daniel Miller sexually abused his daughter. His stomach wrenched at the thought. He cleared his throat, then cleared it again. He decided to change the subject, for now.

"Are you currently dating anyone, Miss Masters?"

"Why, detective. I hardly know you," she quipped. He cocked one eyebrow. "I don't date. I don't like leaving Jenna alone."

"At this point, I've decided not to arrest you. In return, I want to speak to your daughter. I want Jenna to tell me what happened, last night."

Jersey faced him, all softness gone. "I'm sorry, you won't be able to do that."

"Miss Masters, you don't have a choice in this."

"Oh, but I do," she stated.

"No, you don't. In the eyes of the law, a child's welfare is the state's responsibility. If I arrest you, the state will place Jenna in a foster home, and I'll speak to her then."

"Arrest me, detective." Jersey sneered. "Please do. It won't get you what you want. Jenna isn't here."

"Where is she, Miss Masters?" Phillips demanded.

Her laugh mocked him. "That is something you'll only learn with a court order." Jersey walked to the hallway. "If you have no further business, I need to get back to work. Please, show yourself out."

Phillips blew out his frustration on a gruff sigh. At this point, he knew could let her have it, cuffs and all. He didn't need Jenna's body; he only needed a suspicion of foul play. He pictured his niece Alison, vulnerable and frightened. His stomach burned at the thought her daughter suffering at the hands of her father. Though, Jersey hadn't actually said Miller abused his daughter, her body language spoke loud and clear. Because of Alison, he wanted to believe Jersey.

Spencer rinsed his cup at the sink, then went down the hall. He heard Jersey typing through the office door. He thought of sneaking up the stairs, but decided it was too risky. He closed the front door behind him.

Wednesday, November 2

Because Jersey Masters confessed, Phillips moved right to evidence collecting to support her confession. Now, he typed an addendum to his initial report, including Jersey's insinuations against Miller. He knew a prosecutor didn't have to buy her version, however. In eleven year's detective work, he had never hated his job more than today. Collecting evidence against Jersey Masters seemed ludicrous, in light of Miller's crimes. Which meant he believed her allegations, Spencer realized.

Why believe her? Abuse was the don't-blame-me defense of the moment. Everyone had a sob story to tell; childhood traumas caused whatever aberrant behavior had landed them in jail. Spencer snorted. Hucksters, he thought. Degenerates didn't have a clue about real abuse. Then, why believe Jersey Master, he wondered? Because he felt sure Jersey knew abuse firsthand.

And, now, his coffee cup was empty. He stood, stretching generously. Afternoon sun struggled to penetrate the opaque, reinforced windows above him. He headed for the break room via the restroom. When he returned, he found a pink message slip from the Forensics lab on his desk. He set his cup on the desk, slung his brown suit jacket over the back of his chair, then plopped into it. He reached for his phone, punching 4 on the speed dial.

"Forensics. Addison."

"Hey, Nancy. Spencer Phillips here." He put a smile in his voice. Nancy Addison, a statuesque brunette, looked more like a soap star than she did a pathologist. "What have you got?"

"Preliminaries on the Miller shooting. The only blood on the victim belonged to him. He had glass shards embedded in the soles of his shoes, same type as found in the woman's foyer."

"The shooter dropped a bowl of Halloween candy."

"Startled her, huh?" Nancy said.

"That's what she claims."

"Time of death is consistent with the woman's statement. No evidence he was moved after he was shot. The woman is the only one who handled the gun. The decedent's prints are on the outside front door and knob, and on the banister. His prints are not in the master bedroom, or anywhere else downstairs." Nancy breathed. Spencer heard her flipping pages. "No analysis has come back on the vacuum evidence yet. I'm sure we'll find more glass. Pathology samples are, just now, going under the microscope. We'll know more in a couple of hours. The deceased tested negative for alcohol and chemicals."

"Go back to the fingerprints a minute," Spencer said. "Can you say which phone the little girl used to call 911? Or, that she witnessed the altercation between her parents?"

"Little girl? I don't have any child-sized prints in my samples, Spencer."

He clutched the receiver. "Are you sure?"

"Of course, I'm sure. I've got two sets of prints. One: Jersey Masters, homeowner and alleged shooter. Two: Daniel Miller, dead guy. Period."

Uneasiness kicked him. Had Jersey suckered him, after all? "But, the little girl called us. I'm getting her 911 tape, even as we speak."

"I can go over the prints again," Nancy said. "The woman herself has small fingers. It's possible the smaller prints got lost in the others. But, I don't think so."

"Masters has two phones - one in a downstairs office, the other in the master bedroom, upstairs. Check the bedroom phone first. I want to know which one the child used."

"Sure thing. Anything else?"

Spencer saw Rivera hustle into the squad room. "Not yet," he said. "Thanks, Nancy. Bye."

"Here's the 911 tape." Rivera tossed a cassette on Spencer's desk. "Curtis Abbott took the call. He's the department head, so we can count on it's being authentic."

"Good," he said. He snapped the cassette into his portable player. "Let's see what we've got."

Mateo wheeled over a chair and unbuttoned his jacket. Their desks butted each other, situated just off-center of the room. Half a dozen workstations surrounded them. The tape started as the phone rang.

"911 operator, state your emergency."

" 's Daddy," a small voice quavered.

"Your daddy? Has he been hurt? Is he sick?"

Spencer heard the background clicks of a computer keyboard. Abbott had started a trace on the call. As he listened to her voice, Jenna materialized into a real little girl with milk-white skin, her mother's auburn curls and big green eyes. He leaned closer to her.

" 's Daddy, 's Daddy!" Her voice neared hysteria. "I didn't mean it, I didn't!"

"Calm down, honey." Abbott said, his own voice soft and steady. "I'm sure you didn't mean it. Can you tell me what happened?"

She sobbed in reply.

"What's you name, sweetheart?"

"Um." She snuffled. " 's J-Jenna."

"Good. Jenna what?"

"Jenna Miller." She grew calmer, more intelligible.

"How old are you, Jenna?"

"Mm, six."

"What happened to your daddy, Jenna?" Curtis asked, again.

"He—" Her voice broke with tears. She sniffled. "He didn't s'posed to come here. Jersey didn't say he could come here. But, he just did. But, he didn't s'posed to, and—" Her voice soared again. "And, I did kill him with that gun."

"Your father's been shot?"

"Mm hmm."

"Can you tell me if he's breathing, or moving?"

"He's just laying there, where he fell down when—" She started to cry, again.

"Is anyone else in the house with you? A grownup?"

"Jersey's right there on the stairs."

"Jenna, do you live at 418 Presidio Crest Drive?"

"Uh huh. 's Jersey's house," she said.

"Okay, honey. I'm sending someone to help your daddy. Don't hang up until they arrive."

Abbott engaged the child in small talk. Spencer stopped the machine; perspiration beaded his ruddy forehead.

"What do you think, Mateo?"

"I think you're gone on this kid, already." Rivera stripped off his outer ice-gray jacket, revealing a dove gray shirt with white cuffs. "So, the little girl says she shot the old man. The mother's confessed. Who're you going the believe?"

"Jenna is hysterical. Her mother, on the other hand, is pretty calm about the whole matter." Spencer held up both hands, weighing each possibility. "She could be covering for her daughter."

"Or, she has ice in her veins."

"If the father did to his daughter what Masters' claims...."

" 'If' being the operative word, Spence," Rivera interrupted. "Lt. Schoefield doesn't care about 'ifs.' Besides, what Miller did or didn't do to the kid is irrelevant, as far as we're concerned. That's a matter for the defense."

Spencer cupped his face in his hands, exhaling loudly. "I know it, Mateo," he said. "But, this time, it matters to me, damn it. Maybe I've seen one too many child abuse cases, I don't know."

"I know you have, Spence. It's a sick world. But, we're not its doctors, remember? We're just its orderlies, we just clean up the puke."

"Let's put our theories on the table, shall we? I say Jersey Masters killed the father of her child exactly as she said - justifiable homicide."

"She's hiding that kid, that's my bet. An entire neighborhood never saw that six-year-old?"

"I did check out the schools around her home, yesterday. Jenna's not enrolled in any of them."

"Which goes to my theory, right?" Mateo said.

"Keep checking that out. There are lots of private schools in the county. Anything else?"

"Where's the kid, now? Has Masters killed her, too?"

"Tell me why she'd do that?"

"No witness to challenge her version of the shooting."

"But, when did she kill her? After Jenna called us?" Spencer shook his head no. "Jersey Masters is smarter than that."

"Sure she could have." Rivera tapped the metal desktop. "She had twenty minutes to stash the little body, before we got there."

"She dared me to arrest her, yesterday. She said I'd only find Jenna with a court order."

"Then, get the little lady what she asked for." Mateo said. "Call Judge Eichert and Jersey Masters will be in custody before lunch."

"Not yet. If she killed her daughter, I want every T crossed; no questions of her guilt."

"It's your call, Spence. But Schoefield may say otherwise."

"Larry will be my headache. You start discounting my theory; I'll discredit yours."

"You got it." Mateo wheeled away.

Saturday, November 5

"Carol, I can assure you, many arts organizations find fundraising on odious task."

Jersey spoke via speakerphone to the Image Coordinator of the La Mesa Fine Arts League. She pasted a red-and-green elf onto an ad dummy, as she talked, then checked the computer layout.

"Give me you Fax number, Carol. I'll send you my resume, and a proposal for the type of dinner I have in mind."

"Sounds good, Jersey. Here's my number."

She copied the seven digits into her Rolodex, then fed them into her computer. The information sped across the phone lines.

"It looks as good as it sounded," Carol said, minutes later. "Thanks, Jersey. I'll take this before our board on Monday."

Jersey canceled the call, then hit Print. As she turned to the printer, Jenna peeked around the doorway.

"Are you almost done workin' now, Jersey?"

"Not really, Honey Bunny. Why?"

" 'Cause I'm getting hungry for some snack."

"What kind of snack are you getting hungry for?" Jersey laughed. She saved the changes to her layout and exited the file.

"I would, maybe, like some ice cream. Maybe?"

"What kind of ice cream would you 'maybe' like? As if I didn't know."

"I will maybe like some Rocky Road," she said, nodding earnestly.

"I don't think we have any Rocky Road." Jenna looked crestfallen. Jersey grinned. "But, I know where we can get some."

Jenna began to dance. "Oh boy, oh boy. We're gonna get Rocky Road," she sang.

"Let me get my keys, you." Jersey tousled the little girl's golden curls on her way up the stairs.

Forty minutes later, she parked above the cliffs at Ocean Beach. She watched the sun set while Jenna licked her cone and chattered happily.

"I loved Mexico, Jersey. Can we go there again?"

"Sure we can, Honey Bunny." She said, enjoying Jenna's six-year-old exuberance. "Maybe, we'll go next year on your birthday."

"Oh boy!"

Jenna crunched almonds. Jersey smiled again, settling into her seat. Jenna had taken her first plane ride during that trip. That trip might be their only trip, she thought, if Detective Phillips has his way. She allowed herself a memory of last May. Two weeks in Cancun spent sunning on white beaches and swimming in clear waters; souvenir shopping and eating whatever Jenna wanted to try. Jenna's eyes had brought life to the vacation, even the flight home had seemed magical. Jersey leaned back in her car seat, sighing. She had had no idea of the trouble waiting for her at home. The sun dropped into the horizon like a copper penny into a blue silk purse. Jenna munched her sugar cone, dropping crumbs in her lap. Jersey brushed them away and wiped chocolate from her chin.

"Are you through eating?" Jenna nodded. "Good, because I need to talk to you. The police are looking for you, Jenna. I don't want them to find you. So, I need to take you to a safe place. You must stay there, until I come for you."

"Why, Jersey? Are the p'liceman's be putting you in jail?"

Jersey cuddled the child into her side. "That's a possibility, Honey Bunny. I won't lie to you."

"But, I'll tell them, Jersey! I'll tell them I did kill that bad daddy. I'll tell them."

"No, you won't tell them," Jersey stated. She smiled and tweaked Jenna's nose. "Are you trying to do my job?"

Jenna soberly shook her head no.

"Just think of this as a game of hide-and-seek. You are hiding; the police are seeking. As long as they don't find you, we win. Okay?"

"Mm hmm!" Jenna laughed and clapped her hands. "Can I hide now?"

"We're going to do that right now."

The orange sky had gone purple. The ocean roared below them. Jersey switched on the ignition, gunning the engine.

"Put the top down! Put the top down!" Jenna sang.

She shook her head no. "It isn't summertime, any more. Don't forget your seat belt."

She headed out. Jenna leaned her head against the door. Soon, she was fast asleep. Jersey turned up the volume on the radio, humming along with Tony Bennet. She smiled; everything would be fine now.

* * * * *

"Do you think he's comin', yet?" A little girl whispered into the darkness.

Jersey looked toward the sound, but couldn't see anyone. She felt around her; she wasn't in bed any more. She sat, curled against a wall. She pulled her cotton nightgown over her knees, wide-awake now. The floor under her felt smooth and cool to her touch. A balmy air had no fragrance.

"Where am I?" She muttered.

She thought to crawl away. Could she find the little girl who had called her? Something inside her said, "stay put!" The thought petrified her. She peered into the dark.

"Do you think he's comin', yet?" The child whimpered.

"Who?" She whispered back. This was ridiculous, she thought, angrily. Why was she sitting here? Where was the little girl? Who might come?

Suddenly, footsteps walked toward her. Someone in heavy shoes came closer. Fear seized her; Jersey couldn't breathe. The footsteps drew closer still, steady purposeful footfalls. She wanted to run, wanted to scream for help. Her limbs went numb. Her voice locked in her throat. Who would hear her, she wondered, frantically? Little bare feet, on a bare floor, ran passed her. The little girl raced by, shrieking in terror.

Jersey woke hearing her scream. She elbowed herself up. Where was Jenna? She pushed her hair out of her face, listening. No sound came from Jenna's room or anywhere else in the house. Of course not, she berated herself. Jenna was not here; she was safe. Jersey fell back into her pillows. Every night since the shooting she had had a nightmare. Each one like a puzzle piece falling out of a box.

But, I don't have nightmares, she argued. Children have bad dreams. Children, and the weak. Yet, she hadn't stopped them from coming.

"I am not a child," she said, beating her bed covers. "I am not weak. I am strong. I am in control."

Jersey threw off her blankets, jammed her feet into terry scuffs and stomped downstairs. Work. That's what she needed. Work, and a strong cup of coffee.

Monday, November 7

Lieutenant Lawrence Schoefield stormed the squad room. Those who saw him coming scurried for safe ground. Schoefield was a sturdy block of a man with steel gray hair, brushed straight back, and steel gray eyes. He had just gotten off the phone with the district attorney's office. No criminal complaint had been filed on the Miller death. The DA wanted to know why. So did Lt. Schoefield.

"Where's Phillips?" He bellowed.

Six pair of eyes pointed him out. Phillips, in white shirtsleeves, sat at his desk, headphones on, listening to Jenna Miller for the nth time. Her little-girl sobs pierced his heart, again. He didn't see the lieutenant approach. Schoefield planted himself in front of Spencer's desk, jabbing at his headgear. Phillips stripped it off.

"Why haven't you given your report on Miller to the DA?" Schoefield barked.

"It isn't finished yet."

Schoefield reddened. "Why not?"

"I'm not satisfied," Spencer said.

"Satisfied with what? Masters admits killing the guy. What more do you need?"

"I'm not convinced she did it." Spencer cupped his face, spoke through his hands. "On the 911 tape, the little girl says she did it."

"Look, Spence. In the nine years I've known you, your job always has been top priority. It's not like you to throw the law -

not to mention, your career - into the toilet. You said yourself;
she's a baby. She was shaken up."

"Larry, the guy molested his daughter. I'm not crying over his
passing, however it happened."

"It doesn't matter, either way. Police arrest criminals. You're
the police, Masters is the criminal; get satisfied. Get her in here
and get her booked."

"I can't do that yet."

"I can take you off this case. This department literally cannot
afford for you to lose you head over one case."

"Like you said, Larry. You know me. I don't chase rabbits. I
don't go off on tangents. This case is different. Don't ask me to
explain how, just trust me a few more days."

"Let me see the file." Schoefield extended a beefy hand. "What
evidence have you got?"

"Forensic reports, interviews." Spencer handed him the ma-
nila folder. "It's all there."

"Anything conclusive?" Schoefield asked, thumbing pages.

"Miller was shot to death."

"What's the accused's background?"

Spencer tossed his headset on the desk. "Until now, Masters
was a model citizen. Nothing more than a parking ticket, which
she paid. She's quiet; her neighbors hardly know her. She has a
good reputation in the business community as a top-notch public
relations rep."

"It's always the quiet ones, isn't it?" Schoefield grimaced. "Because I know you, you've got the time. Not much, though. I've got
superiors, too."

As the lieutenant stalked away, Mateo wheeled over. Today, he
wore a toast-colored jacket over lime-green pants. He had a different suit for every day of the week, Spencer thought. He, himself,
owned two sport coats - one brown, one blue - with two pair of
trousers apiece. Spencer's dark blue sport coat hung from the back
of his chair.

"Schoefield's pretty steamed, huh?"

Spencer nodded, twisting his headphones between his fingers. "He thinks I've lost my objectivity where Jersey Masters is concerned."

"It's not the mother, Spence. It's her kid. What's going on with you?"

"I believe the woman." Phillips shrugged. "When she says Miller abused his daughter, I believe her. When she says she didn't expect him that night, I believe her."

"Did she say he abused the girl?" Rivera asked. "You have doubts."

"Not doubts, just concerns. Why hasn't anyone seen this little girl?" He said, tapping the tape player. "We canvassed the entire neighborhood. No one even knew Jersey Masters had a daughter. There are no school records anywhere in town for a Jenna Miller, either. Why?"

"Miller made no legal claim to the girl, not in San Diego anyway. Still, it's not too hard to believe Masters is lying, is it?" Mateo asked. "People lie to the police, you know."

Spencer shook his head, cupping his face in his hands.

"Have you reconsidered the possibility that Masters got rid of the girl?"

"The thought crossed my mind," Phillips admitted.

"If you even suspect she's harmed that child, you have to move, Spence. You can't wait."

"I know, I know. Except, Jenna Miller has been a mystery all along. She didn't disappear yesterday, Mateo. It's as if she never existed."

"Jersey Masters created a child from whole cloth?" Rivera exclaimed. "She is a nut case."

"But, we have the girl's voice. And, I've seen Masters' home. It certainly looks as if a child lives there."

"We've got loons coming out the wall sockets, around here. Everyone's a schizophrenic."

"Find me a birth certificate, Mateo. If Jenna Miller was born, she has a birth certificate. Find it."

"You've got it."

Rivera saluted him, then rolled back to his desk. Phillips stared down at the Masters file. If Jersey concocted a daughter, then why had Miller come a thousand miles to see her? He thought about Daniel Miller, now. His driver's license listed his date of birth as 1939. He was fifty-six years old; Jersey was twenty-seven. Was he a man in a mid-life crisis?

He wondered if Miller had a family, a wife and/or children? Rivera had noted his contact with Nevada police. They would have notified any family. Spencer shuffled through the file until he found Miller's address, but no phone number. He phoned the 702 operator and penciled Miller's home number into the margin. He mashed buttons. The other line rang seven times. Spencer almost hung up.

"Hello?" A young man said.

"Is this the Daniel Miller residence of Carson City, Nevada?"

"Uh, yes it is. Who's this?"

"Detective Spencer Phillips of the San Diego Police Department. Am I speaking to Mr. Miller's son?"

"Uh, yes." The boy hesitated. "I'm Kurt Miller."

"Please don't be alarmed, son. I'm a homicide detective working your Dad's case. Is you mother at home, Kurt?"

"Uh, yeah. But, she's lying down. I'll see if she wants to talk to you."

"Thank you, son."

Waiting, Spencer heard the hollow echo of family life. MTV, or a heavy metal radio station, pounded in the background. A clothes dryer hummed. He imagined the Miller's kitchen, jotting notes into the file. After several minutes, he heard footsteps approach. A woman answered, sounding tired and drained. He identified himself again.

"I apologize for troubling you, ma'am," he said. "I wondered if I could ask you some follow-up questions." She hesitated, as her son had, before agreeing. "How long were you and Mr. Miller married?"

"Sixteen years." Her voice wavered.

Confirmed, Spencer thought. Miller's relationship with Jersey had been an extramarital one. He sympathized with the widow. "I'm sure the Nevada police have asked you all these questions. I apologize for the repetition."

"I'm sure you're only doing your job." Mrs. Miller sighed.

"Why was your husband in San Diego, Halloween night?"

"Looking for his daughter. He wasn't even sure she lived there. None of his attempts to contact her had succeeded. But, he had to try."

"You knew about your husband's relationship with Jersey Masters?" His voice echoed his surprise.

"The woman who killed him? Oh no, I'd never heard of her until the police called that night."

"Then, you didn't know she was Jenna's mother?"

"No. Daniel only told me about his daughters. He felt ashamed about deserting them. They were both so little. He worked for more than a year relocating each of them."

"Them!" His chest constricted. "Two girl? Twins?"

"Oh, no. Jenna is the older of the two girls."

"Where is his other daughter, now?" He asked, chiding himself. Men who cheated, often made it a habit.

"She lives in Northern California. In fact, she told Daniel where to find Jenna."

"How's that?" His stomach acid boiled.

"She gave him Jenna's address and phone number."

"You mean the two families know each other?"

"I assume so," she said. "I don't know much about my husband's life before I met him. Daniel didn't like to talk of it."

There appeared to be a lot he didn't like to talk about, Spencer thought. "Do you have an address for the sister?"

"No, I wish I did. The poor thing may never know her father is dead."

"Mrs. Miller, you said your husband searched more than a year for Jenna. When, exactly, did he locate each of his daughters?"

She sighed, again. "He found Patrice right away. She was so glad to hear from him, after so long. The two spent several weekends together. I think that was in February, or March of this year."

"And, he found Jenna last month?"

"That's when Daniel went to see her, yes. He first tried to contact her in May, using the information he got from her sister. He left a message on an answering machine, then he wrote several letters."

Spencer cupped his face in his free hand, stunned. He couldn't believe it. Masters had lied to him. His instincts had failed him.

"That was in May?" He asked. His gut churned as she confirmed it was. "Mrs. Miller, you should be aware.... Jersey Masters has alleged your husband...sexually abused her daughter."

"What!" She gasped. "That's crazy. My husband would never harm a child in that way. How dare she make such a horrible accusation? Surely, you won't let the spiteful ravings of a murderer taint my husband's good name."

Phillips listened with his instincts. If he had to put money on the veracity of Miller's wife or his daughter, he chose Jenna. But, Jenna hadn't made the allegations, her mother had. Jersey's veracity was less than stellar, especially after this conversation. He couldn't think of anything more to ask. His whole thought digested the fact that Jersey had lied to him.

"Thank you very much, for your time," he said, absently. "I apologize again for disturbing you, in your grief."

"I hope I've helped you," she said. "I'm not a vindictive woman, by nature. But, I hope Miss Masters -. Never mind. Good bye, detective."

Spencer ignored the dial tone. He was stunned, mortified. The green-eyed witch had duped him. He had swallowed every spoonful of her story, jeopardizing his career for nothing. He banged the receiver against his forehead. Think, he ordered. Analyze the facts. The ramifications were devastating. If he was wrong -.

Suppose Jersey wasn't lying. Miller could be capable of the despicable act Jersey accused him of. Molesters looked like everyone else, and they didn't stop with one victim. If Miller got off on kids, Phillips reasoned, there could have been others. How could he find out? Who else could he contact about Miller's alleged predilections? Who might know?

Miller's son, of course, if Miller molested him and if he would talk about it. Would his mother let him talk about it? Probably not, judging by her earlier reaction to the subject.

Jenna's sister...what was her name? Patrice! She might know, supposing he could find her, and supposing her mother allowed him to ask. Maybe, Patrice's mother knew and was just as angry as Jersey, he thought. He drew a large question mark beside Patrice's name.

He could check doctors and hospitals in San Diego and Carson City, to see if any had treated or admitted Miller's children. Assuming Miller's name was used in connection with the children. Assuming, too, doctors would breach confidentiality, especially with no confirmed abuse.

He flipped through his notes, again. CalID, the state's fingerprint database, had kicked back Miller's criminal record. Two assault-and-battery charges filed in 1969; both dropped. A restraining order issued in 1973; granted to a Marguerite Wilson. Patrice's mother, he wondered? No evidence Miller had violated the order. With a giant stretch of his imagination, he could infer Wilson brought the order to protect Patrice from her father's sick pleasures.

Phillips shook his head. No judge in any court would take his inferences as fact. He stood, slid into his jacket and pocketed his notebook. He would go to her house. When he returned, he would have concrete answers. Or, he would have Jersey Masters in handcuffs.

Monday, November 7

Jersey lifted a grocery bag from her car trunk and hurried toward the house. With Jenna gone, she felt lonely. Jenna's constant pleas for this or that treat made grocery shopping more fun. Her beguiling smile was irresistible. But, Jenna couldn't be out and about, she told herself.

The smooth white driveway led her to a red-poured patio with potted azaleas and succulents in cedar planters. A neatly groomed backyard encircled the house. The red wooden doors of a detached garage were shut tight. Jersey shifted the bag to her hip and unlocked the kitchen door. Over her shoulder, she saw Detective Phillips round the corner carrying her other sack. She pushed the door open with her toe and shifted the weight in her arms to face him. He looked furious. Her expression remained placid.

"Detective Phillips, do come in."

"I intend to, Miss Masters," he replied, crisply. "You have some explaining to do."

He followed her into the spotless kitchen. Jersey instructed him to set the bag on a counter. She began to unpack groceries as if he weren't standing behind her. He watched for several minutes, awed by her implacability. A half pot of vanilla coffee perfumed the air. She wore a hunter green sweater over black patterned leggings and a pair of chunky work boots. Her face and hair looked flawless. She moved like a woman with no cares. Spencer peered into the bag at his elbow, inventorying its contents - a honey-roasted cereal, a devil's food cake mix, frozen fudge pops— Jersey pulled the bag away.

"I know all about it," he declared.

"Well, good for you." Jersey stowed perishables in her refrigerator and turned. "What is it you know?"

"I talked to Millers' wife this morning. She told me he first contacted you in May. She said he phoned and wrote you repeatedly over the last six months."

"She's lying." Jersey shrugged.

"She's lying! Why would she lie?"

"Because she can't face the truth. Maybe, she doesn't even know what the truth is."

"What truth doesn't she know? You think she doesn't know that you had an affair with her husband? Oh, she knows that truth. She's known for some time."

Contempt hardened her eyes. "A woman couldn't satisfy that bastard. He took a child for his mistress."

Her statement knocked the anger from him. Spencer cupped his face in his hands, then dropped them. Unfathomable emotion flushed his face and neck.

"The man had a family, for Pete's sake."

"Oh, my God!" Jersey froze. "He had other children? Did he.... Has he hurt any of them?"

"Not that I know of," Spencer said.

"Not that you know of?" She mocked. "Did you ask?"

He admitted he had not. Jersey turned away, disgusted.

"Did you lie about Miller contacting you, prior to Halloween night?"

"Yes, I lied," she huffed, shaking her head. "I had to. I can't take care of Jenna from a jail cell."

He spun her around by her shoulder. "By God, you had better tell me the truth now, or that's exactly where you will be."

Jersey sank into a kitchen chair. She rested her chin in her hand, searching the walnut tabletop. She dropped her hand onto the table, tracing the leaf crease with her thumbnail. Spencer leaned against the counter.

"The first call came on my birthday, May 15. Jenna and I had just returned from a vacation in Mexico. I carried Jenna to bed and brought in our suitcases, then I settled in. His voice came out of my answering machine like a cold wave; telling Jenna how he'd never stopped loving her. I yanked the tape from my machine and smashed it to pieces with a hammer. Jenna saw me and asked what I was doing. I never told her what was on the tape." Jersey looked up at the detective.

"She soon forgot about it. He didn't call again for a couple of months. I hoped he would think he had the wrong number. I only wish I'd had the forethought to call him and tell him it was the wrong number, before I smashed that tape."

"But, he called back?"

Jersey nodded. "He said Patrice had given him my number, so he knew it was right. I couldn't believe it was him. After so many years, I never expected to hear from him again."

"How many times did he call you, over the last six months?"

"He called once a week." She scoffed. "I never returned a single one. I burned every letter, unopened."

"Do you have an attorney, Miss Masters?"

"Yes, why?"

He straightened and came toward her. "As an officer of the state of California, I am placing you under arrest for the shooting death of Daniel Miller."

"You're what?"

"I should have arrested you the night of the shooting. In light of what you've just told me, I have no other choice. In a moment, I'll read you your rights. You need to hear and understand them, thoroughly. I will allow you to call your attorney from here, before I take you in."

"May I bring my briefcase?" Jersey asked. "I have work that must be done this afternoon."

Phillips shook his head no.

"Deadlines are my business, detective. If I can't meet my deadlines, I'm out of business."

"All right, bring it with you," he said. "I'll try to get it to you later. I can't promise, though."

He followed her to her study, watched as she made her call and gathered her work into a leather attaché. When she finished, he withdrew a set of handcuffs.

"Please hold out your wrists," he said.

Monday, November 7

An hour later, Jersey stood before a stainless steel sink and commode unit, trying to wash the gritty fingerprint ink off her fingers. The two-tone, mustard and butter walls of her cell were thick from frequent painting. Two metal bunks were bolted to the left wall. A matron had given her a thin mattress; the slick plastic ticking stank of disinfectant. Jersey wore her street clothes - sweater and leggings. She dried her hands on her hips.

Never in her wildest imagination had she expected to be jailed for killing Daniel Miller. He deserved to die for what he'd done, she thought. Jenna was his victim. The child couldn't defend herself, in the face of such evil. At best, Jersey considered shooting him self-defense; at worst, killing him was retribution for his crimes.

Should she not have killed him, she asked herself? Should she have stood by while he assaulted Jenna again? Yet, because she pulled the trigger she was the criminal and he was the victim. Jersey paced her cell, her arms folded across her chest, growing angrier as her mind worked. Anger served no purpose, she cautioned herself. She couldn't afford to lose her composure, but she couldn't let go of the bitterness.

Across the street, Spencer listened again as Jenna told Curtis Abbott that she killed her father. A schism of victory shot through him, but it wasn't enough to burn off his frustration. Mrs. Miller had confirmed the child's existence. Her husband had come to San Diego to find Jenna. So, why could he find no record of her?

Why had no one ever seen her? And, where was she now? He sighed, exasperated.

The Masters woman was an enigma. She rode in the back of his car; her shoulders straight, her hands folded in her lap, as if he were a chauffeur rather than her arresting office. She cooperated fully throughout the booking process, her posture erect, her head high. Even when he presented her with a copy of her previous statement, she gave no clues - verbal or nonverbal - suggesting she hadn't been completely honest all along.

At his elbow, the phone rang. He looped his headphones around his neck and lifted the receiver. "Spence, it's Rivera. I've got a neighbor who's not only seen Jenna Miller, she talked to the kid."

"She's talked to Jenna!" His heart dipped and leapt. "Will she talk to us?"

Rivera cupped the receiver, relaying the request. "She'll come," he said. "We'll be in the office in twenty."

Spencer slam-dunked his receiver, and pumped the air. Yes! A scrap of success, at last. He had never worked a more frustrating case. Jersey Masters fascinated him as much as she infuriated him. The average citizen found the booking process a nerve-wracking experience. Yet, she appeared no more harassed than had she been renewing her driver's license. She had brevity of words and gestures that was maddening. She wasted neither. She either was the strongest woman he had ever met, or the most brilliant actress, he thought. Even so, he couldn't imagine her as a murderer.

"She's here, Spence." Rivera broke his reverie. "Interview Three. I've let Schoefield know she's here. He's meeting us downstairs. I knew he'd want to sit in."

"Marsha, we'll need you, again."

Spencer leapt from his seat, snatching his jacket from its back. The female officer hurried after the two detectives.

"The witness's name is Suzanne Kirby. She lives right next door to Masters. She just returned this morning from a medical symposium in New York City. She says she spent about an hour with the little girl last Christmas."

Lt. Schoefield waited outside Interview Room Three. He looked noncommittal. Spencer entered first, then Schoefield, Rivera and Marsha. The room itself was a mere cubicle. Fresh paint and new carpet had eradicated most of the stink and stain left over from the years before the no-smoking ordinances. Suzanne Kirby was a slim black woman, professional in dress and manner. She sat on a plastic molded chair at a small wooden table. She hadn't removed her coat, an umbrella dripped on the floor. Spencer introduced his entourage and thanked her for coming.

"May I offer you coffee?"

"Thank you, no," she said. "I'd just like to tell you what I know and be on my way."

"That's fine." Spencer placed a tape recorder between them, and pressed Record. He recited the preliminaries, then looked at her. "Detective Rivera tells us you met Jenna Miller last Christmas, correct?" His notepad was open, his pen poised.

"Yes, it is."

"How did the encounter come about?" Mateo asked.

"Let me ask you something, first," Ms. Kirby said, to Spencer. "Is Miss Masters in trouble for shooting that man?"

"Ms. Kirby," Schoefield spoke up. "A man is dead, and she says she shot him. One couldn't be in more trouble."

"We need all the facts to make a fair determination," Spencer said.

"I won't be a party to putting her in jail. I could have killed himself myself, after what he did to his daughter."

"You have knowledge of Jenna's abuse by her father?" Spencer's gut began to churn.

"Not firsthand knowledge, no. But, I saw its effect. Her father was a pig."

Schoefield cleared his throat, a warning to tread lightly. Spencer cupped his hands, dropping them with an audible sigh. Without firsthand knowledge, Ms. Kirby's suspicions were just that, and were inadmissible.

"Please tell us everything you know, firsthand, about Jersey

Master, Jenna Miller and her father." He said.

Ms. Kirby lifted her shoulders. "I never met Jenna's father, and I knew Jersey only slightly. We met a couple of years ago when she borrowed an egg. She said she was baking a birthday cake and had dropped her last one. I wished her 'Happy Birthday' and she told me it was Jenna's birthday. Until then, I didn't know she had a child. I watched for her, but I didn't see her. Not until last Christmas, that is."

"How did that come about?" Spencer asked, enthralled by this woman bringing Jenna to life.

"She came running out of her house, crying terribly."

"The little girl, or her mother?" Mateo interrupted.

"It was Jenna," she assured them. "She had cut her hand. It was bleeding pretty bad, and she was near hysteria."

"Did she say where her mother was?" Spencer asked.

"No, and I didn't think to ask," Ms. Kirby said. "I brought the child into my home and made her some cocoa, trying to calm her. The poor thing only had on her nightgown. I cleaned the cut, which wasn't as bad as it looked. When she calmed down, I asked her name and how old she was. Jenna said she cut her hand on a broken ornament. All that blood had terrified her. She was a sweet child. I enjoyed meeting her."

Spencer glanced up from his notes. "Can you give us a physical description of the girl, Ms. Kirby?"

"The child looks like Jersey Masters, detective."

"When did she tell you her father molested her?" Schoefield asked.

"I'm a clinical psychologist, detectives. That child didn't have to tell me her father molested her. I could see it for myself."

"I don't understand," Spencer said.

"I'm invoking patient/therapist confidentiality, now." She gathered her belongings and got to her feet. "If you want to understand any more, you will have to speak to Miss Masters. To know Jersey is to know Jenna. I cannot tell you more than that. Good afternoon, gentlemen."

"One moment, Ms. Kirby," Rivera said. "We'll need you to sign your statement before a notary public downstairs. I'll ask the clerk to rush the paperwork. It shouldn't take more than thirty minutes. Officer Marsha Reed, here, will show you where to wait."

The two women left, and Schoefield lowered his bulk into the plastic chair Suzanne Kirby had just vacated. Rivera joined them at the table. The three men spoke, simultaneously.

"So, you have your witness," Schoefield said. "For the defense."

"Okay, the kid exists." Mateo conceded. "But, it doesn't rule her mom out for a rubber room."

"What did she mean, 'to know Jersey is to know Jenna'?" Spencer wondered, aloud.

"This Masters woman killed the father of her child." Schoefield slammed his hand on the table. "What was her motive, Rivera? Spencer, where are your witnesses? Why don't you two have any solid leads? I want answers. I don't want this gal to walk."

"Child abuse, that was her motive," Phillips said.

"Spence, you got no concrete on that," Mateo said. "Masters is a virtual stranger to her own neighbors. She's not only hiding her daughter, she's hiding herself."

"Go get that gal." Schoefield jabbed his finger at Spencer. "Keep on her until she tells you what you want to know."

* * * * *

Jersey perched on the bottom bunk. Sounds drifted through the metal bars of her cell. Other prisoners laughed or cursed; someone flushed a toilet. Officers jangled keys, slid open heavy doors and slammed them shut again. Solid footsteps approached her cell and Jersey's stomach flip-flopped. A heavy, black woman in navy blue polyester said, "Follow me. You got a friend to see ya."

She led Jersey to a small conference room where her friend Deborah Wailey waited at a gray metal table. Jersey slid into the other seat. The officer locked the grilled door, behind her.

"Thanks for coming, Deborah," she said. "I admit, I'm surprised to see you."

Spencer checked Ms. Kirby's progress, then headed across the street to county lock-up. Apprehension settled over him like a wet blanket. He pushed through the outer doors where the attending officer greeted him warmly. He signed the visitor's roster, writing Jersey Masters' name under Prisoner to See. Officer Roxbury shook her head, seeing the name, informing him the prisoner already had a visitor.

"I'll wait," he said, and Roxbury buzzed him through.

Spencer positioned a chair outside the visitor's conference room where he could see the two women. He recognized Deborah Wailey, Metro editor for the San Diego Union-Tribune, and wondered why the press was interested in Masters. The editor was of medium build; mid-forties with long black hair pinned back from her sallow face with a gold barrette. She looked distressed, attending to Jersey in maternal fashion.

"I couldn't believe it when I saw the news brief on you." Wailey said. "You, of all people, arrested for manslaughter. What happened?"

"I don't know that I want to talk about it." Jersey swept away a stray brown curl. "Not to you, no offense. I don't need any more publicity."

"How long have we worked together, Jersey? Three years? Four? You're one of the most reliable publicists I've ever worked with. I'm not here to pry, but the story will come out. As your friend, I can make sure it's accurate, from your point of view."

"What do you know, already?"

Spencer leaned forward, curious. The Metro editor repeated everything she had read in the beat report, sketchy as it was. She asked Jersey about her relationship with Miller and Spencer tipped his chair even closer. Jersey retold her story, omitting all references to Jenna or Miller's abuse. Wailey scribbled every word on a yellow pad.

"You believed he was after you, that's why you shot him?"

Jersey nodded. "This is more of the same stuff we report every day. People aren't safe in their own homes."

"And, when I fought back, I ended up in jail."

Spencer sat back, folding his arms across his chest, smiling ruefully.

"This makes good press," Wailey said. "It should draw plenty of public opinion to your case, too."

"Don't tell me about public opinion," Jersey said. "I manipulate public opinion in every campaign I produce. It doesn't guarantee anything, especially in a court of law."

"Stranger things, etc." Deborah said. "I'll bring you a copy of your story, okay?"

The women rose together. Jersey extended her hand. Deborah embraced it warmly, looking as if she wanted to hug Jersey. As they passed him, Jersey smirked at Spencer. A matron halted Jersey at the door. Deborah squeezed her hand again, and left. Spencer clasped her elbow, feeling guilty for having eavesdropped, and led her back to the table.

Wednesday, November 9

At 8:30 a.m., a young man in a gray wool suit presented his credentials at the window of county lock-up.

"Good morning," he said, flashing perfect teeth. "I'm Cary Dodd, counsel for Jersey Masters. I'd like to see my client."

The duty officer scrutinized his identification, then his clean cut, blonde hair and blue eyes. Once inside, officers searched his briefcases, issued him a visitor's pass and directed him to a conference room that reeked of new carpet over old crimes where he waited. Jersey came in, looking dreadful in blue polyester. She had tied her hair into a puffy ponytail and scrubbed her face of makeup. They shook hands. Jersey returned his smile without hesitation. He apologized for having been unavailable during booking. He cited work; she assured him she understood. They sat and he placed a white legal pad and a Bic stick before each of them. Without preamble, he began.

"Jersey, you'll be charged with manslaughter in the first degree; a class B felony, punishable be twenty-five years in prison, if you're found guilty. I've read your statements to the police. I wish you hadn't made them without me. It's my belief, however, that we have a strong case for justifiable homicide. That's what we'll try for. Now, I'd like you to take me through that night, minute by minute."

Jersey pressed her back into her chair, raising her chin. Their professional relationship went back several years, but she debated how far to trust him.

"It was Halloween, Cary. Kids had been ringing my doorbell for hours. So, I wasn't checking before I opened my door. If I had, I wouldn't have opened it so readily."

"Did Miller tell you why he was there?"

She hesitated, thinking back. "He said he had been trying to reach me for weeks. I told him we had nothing to say to each other, and I told him to leave. Instead, he walked into my house."

"You were clear about wanting him to leave?"

"Very," Jersey said.

"How many times did you have to make that request?"

Jersey rubbed her forehead with her fingertips. "Four or five times, I think. Each time, he came further in."

"Saying what?"

"Oh, uh." She blew out a sigh, remembering. " 'Why didn't you return my calls.' 'I don't understand.' 'Why won't you talk to me?' "

"Why wouldn't you talk to him?"

"He had nothing to say that I cared to hear."

"Did he threaten you?"

"Not verbally, no. He came into my house, uninvited, and repeatedly refused to leave. How threatening did he have to be, for Christ's sake, before I could protect myself?"

"According to the law, pretty damn threatening." Cary said. "Where was Miller when you warned him about the gun?"

"At the bottom of the stairs, I think. I had started up, and he followed me."

"And, he said —?"

"He wanted to talk." She stressed the word talk with disgust.

"Meaning, you thought he wanted something else?"

"I knew he wanted something else. I wasn't about to let him have it."

"What did you think he wanted?"

Jersey lowered her lashes. Her cheeks flamed, her chest labored. Cary focused on his notes, feeling like a voyeur.

"Okay," he said. "You ran to your bedroom, you got your gun, then what?"

"I stepped into the hall. He was halfway across the landing, walking away from me. I pointed the gun at him and ordered him to stop. He turned around, saw the gun and came at me."

"He came at you, while you were holding a gun?"

"I thought so. He had his hands up, like this -." She demonstrated; palms out, fingers splayed. "I thought he meant to grab me. I panicked and fired the gun."

"On November first, you talked to a Detective Phillips in your home. Your statements to him were extremely vague. I imagine he let you get away with it because no lawyer was present. Tell me what you didn't tell him, that day. You need to be completely honest with me."

Jersey paused, sorting her options. Complete honesty could get her into more trouble, she knew. If her answers weren't consistent, he would want to know why. She sighed again.

"What do you think I left out?" She hedged.

"Describe your relationship with Daniel Miller."

"We slept together."

"Did he ever promise you more?"

"He promised me everything. He just never delivered."

"Did that make you bitter?" Cary asked. "Bitter enough to kill him?"

"Of course not. He didn't have anything I wanted. I was so relieved when he left. I hoped I'd never see him again. He disgusted me."

"Is that why you killed him, because he disgusted you?"

"In a manner of speaking," she said, staring at the blank white pad.

"How long did you and Miller sleep together?"

"Three or four years, I think."

"That's a long time. Long enough to know him pretty well. You inferred Miller abused your daughter. Is that the truth?"

"Yes, it is!"

"How old was Jenna when he first molested her?"

"I'm not sure." She paused, her brows knit together.

"But, you're sure he molested her?" Cary pressed forward, scrutinizing her face. Jersey nodded, shielding her eyes with thick lashes. He pursed his lips. "You're sure?"

"I—" Jersey bit her lip; humiliation scorched her cheeks. "I saw him."

Cary dropped his pen. "You saw him! What did you do?"

"I stopped it," she said, shielding herself with her arms. "He didn't molest her again, as long as I could help it."

His heart hammered in his chest. Cary longed to reach across the table and comfort her. But Jersey's expression forbade any overtures.

"Did you seek medical attention for Jenna?"

"She saw a doctor once, as I remember. He said Jenna as so young, she'd probably forget all about it."

"Modern medicine." Cary scoffed. "When was the last time you saw Miller?"

"Halloween night."

"That's not what I meant."

"I know." A curious light grew in her eyes.

"Then, tell me the truth."

Jersey tossed her head, her green eyes hardening to jade. "Time is such a subjective measure, isn't it?" She said, glibly. "For me, it's been years and years since that bastard left. For Jenna, it's only been a few days."

"You left out a very crucial person from your statement, Jersey. Where was Jenna during the shooting?" Cary rolled his pen between his fingers. It clicked against his wedding band.

"Listen to me carefully." She leaned her forearms on the table, leveling him with her gaze. "Jenna has nothing do with what happened, that night. I do not want her involved."

"With Jenna, we have a strong case for self-defense," he said, matching her regard. "Providing she saw what you say happened. Without her, my job gets harder. I don't like my job made harder."

"I'm sorry, Cary. I won't allow you to bring her into this."

"You may not have a choice. The district attorney has raised questions, already. She insists on knowing where your daughter is. She's hinted at criminal action, if you continue to block her efforts to speak to Jenna. She's even speculated you harmed Jenna."

"That's absurd!" Jersey snapped. "Why would I harm Jenna?"

"To prevent her from telling the truth."

"Which would make sense if I claimed to be innocent. But, I don't. Cary, I freely admit shooting him."

"But, you also said he provoked you. And, you've accused Miller of sexual abuse. The prosecution may allege you concocted that story to justify killing a man who only wanted to see his child."

Jersey set her jaw. "The district attorney must prove her allegations, just as I must prove mine."

"She doesn't need any proof to charge you with harming your daughter. Miller's wife says he came here to reconnect with Jenna. And, the judge can deny you bail."

"I'll take my chances," she said, shrugging.

"My point is, with Jenna's corroboration you don't have to take any chances." Cary drummed his fingers on the gray table.

"No."

He blew out air, exasperated. "Will you at least tell me where Jenna is, so I can assure the judge she's safe?"

Jersey glanced to her right, then back at him. "I'm supposed to go home to Santa Cruz for Thanksgiving," she said. "Do you think that will be possible?"

"Thank you." Cary grabbed his briefcases and stuffed his legal pad into one. "You'll be arraigned Friday afternoon, at two o'clock. Is there anything specific you want to wear?"

"I do have a killer red suit that looks positively wicked." She grinned.

"That's the Jersey Masters I know and love." Cary chuckled. "Make me a list. I'll go by your house this afternoon and bring your things to you later."

Thursday, November 10

Spencer sat in early morning traffic, his mind racing ahead of him. Nancy still had found no child-sized prints, so today he planned to dust Jenna's bedroom himself. Rivera was meeting him at the Masters' house with a search warrant, in an hour. Spencer didn't know what they would find. Jersey had blocked his every attempt to see or speak to her little girl. No school records, no birth records for Jenna Miller; the litany echoed in his head. Why? What was she hiding?

His thoughts chased each other as he chased bumpers on Highway 163. He ignored the verdant hills, studded with palms, and the century-old bridges that made this one of the oldest and most beautiful highways in California. Nearing junction 8, cars began to bottleneck. Spencer gridlocked with hundreds of other workers hurrying to punch in by nine. He slammed his hand on the steering wheel, inadvertently blowing his horn. A biker next to him glanced over. Spencer waved sheepishly. The biker waved back with his middle finger. Mercifully, traffic advanced. Spencer exited at Friars Road and drove around Old Town, toward Presidio Crest Drive. No school records, no birth records, he thought again. Why?

He parked his plain brown sedan behind Jersey's midnight-blue Mustang, and surveyed the exterior of her house. Anyone observing him, in his plain brown suit might mistake him for a real estate appraiser. The outside of a home introduced its occupants. Neatly manicured grounds denoted money, just as threadbare grass and weed-choked shrubs conveyed poverty. Bikes and toys meant active children resided on the premises. Jersey's deep green lawn looked well kept, but showed no trace of the child who supposedly lived there.

Spencer examined her car, next. Both doors were locked. He could unfasten the canvas top, he thought, and make a thorough search. But, wrestling with the cover was sure to attract neighbors. Spencer peered through the windows, instead. No food wrappers or papers cluttered the cream interior. Its neatness didn't surprise him.

He walked up the driveway, around to the patio. Plastic covered the bare redwood furniture, protecting it from winter storms and salt air. Mats at both doors harbored no key; neither did the doorjambs or any of the potted plants. Jersey was not a reckless woman, Spencer thought. Glancing about, he withdrew a credit card from his wallet, too impatient to wait for Rivera and the key, then jimmied open the French doors and slipped into the dining room.

Spencer leaned against the doors, still grasping the knobs, adjusting to the dimness of the room. Technically, this was breaking and entering, he thought. But, he was too frustrated to care. He should wait for Rivera, he knew. They had a lot of work to do and his actions tainted any evidence he discovered now. He realized he was holding his breath, and released it, chiding himself. Had he expected to find Jenna's lifeless body lying on the dining table? Over the back of the couch, he spotted a small blonde head, sitting motionless. Jenna? Spencer dashed across the room, his heart racing.

"Jenna?" Spencer leaned over the sofa and laughed. My Size Barbie smiled vacuously at him.

He walked to the kitchen, his limbs quaking with relief. Stepping into her kitchen was like stepping into a Mexican café, he thought. He ran his hand over a counter. Spotless counters, spotless appliances, spotless floor; did Jersey ever use the room, he wondered?

Her cupboards yielded kid-pleasing cereals, canned pastas and snacks, alongside adult equivalents. Her freezer kept two full ice trays frozen, a five-pound bag of Mexican coffee and a pint of Ben and Jerry's Smooth Chocolate ice cream, half-eaten. He shut the door, realizing he'd anticipated finding body parts neatly wrapped and labeled. The thought revolted him. This job was making him psychotic and cynical, he thought.

Spencer strode down the hall, his heels beating the tiles, to Jersey's study. The telephone bleated as he opened the door, startling him. He froze in the doorway, clutching the knob. Jersey's voice answered after four rings; thanked the caller for calling Creative Image Masters and gave further instructions. Spencer ignored the phone and surveyed the room. He imagined Jersey working behind the cherry desk, surrounded by ferns and palms. He saw her slim fingers poised above her computer keyboard, her vivid eyes following a line of text across the screen. What truths did she hide behind that implacable façade?

"Miss Masters," a woman's voice said. "This is Brenda at Pacific Security. I'm notifying police that you've not responded to —"

Spencer grabbed up the receiver. "This is Detective Spencer Phillips with San Diego Police. We're already on the scene, Miss, uh, Brenda."

She hesitated. "You're a police officer?"

"Yes, ma'am. Detective Spencer Phillips, homicide division. We have a search warrant."

"Why didn't you deactivate the security system?"

"My partner should have done so. I'll find him and take care of it."

"Could I have you badge number for our records?" She asked.

Spencer recited his I.D. number, feeling his ears redden. He heard her enter it into her computer. She instructed him to turn off the system right away.

"If I can't find my partner, can you give me the code?"

"No, I can't." She said, irritably.

"Thank you," he said, berating himself. He knew she wouldn't give him that information, and now he'd probably tipped his hand. "Miss Masters will be glad to hear you do you job so well."

He dropped the phone in its cradle, guilt gnawing his intestines. Brenda hadn't sounded convinced, but, then, he hadn't sounded convincing. If she called the station to verify his story, Schoefield would surely want to know why he was here an hour early. Spencer frowned at the intrusive machine. The citrine message light winked back. He pursed his lips and rewound the tape. Two clients wondered why Jersey had not contacted them as promised. Spencer spied a cube of rainbow paper, then vetoed the idea of writing down the messages. Better to find them later, with Rivera present.

"Hi, Jersey! 's Jenna. Am I comin' home, yet? I like to play here, but I will like to play with my own toys better. I like it when I'm sleeping in my own bed, too. So, I want to come home now, I think. 'Kay?"

Her voice stopped. Jenna was still alive! Relief flooded him, surprising him at the same time. Spencer played the tape, again, his heart pounding. He wore a perspiration mustache. After a third run-through, he took the cassette from the machine, inserted it into a player with dubbing capabilities on a nearby credenza and added Jenna's message to his copy of Suzanne Kirby's interview. He returned the original cassette to the answering machine and pocketed his tape.

He pushed aside nagging thoughts of poisoned fruit and continued searching her desk. Jersey's Rolodex was filled with names followed by titles like Director of Publications and Creative Marketing. Her "in" basket held three newspaper business sections and a flier for an upcoming trade show at the San Diego Convention Center; her "out" basket was empty. Deadlines, appointments and a fundraiser for a local hospital loaded her desk calendar. Her wastebasket was empty.

He booted her computer, but Jersey had a password. After trying the usual combinations without success, he turned it off again. Her desk drawers were locked, as were her file cabinets. Spencer searched likely hiding places for a key, to no avail. Damn! A real burglar would have quite a run for his money.

An odd little table drew his attention. It was the only clutter in the room. Bits and letters clung to the table edges. A switch on the table's side illuminated an old advertising layout from underneath. He admired her work, wondering how many of her ads he had seen without knowing it. He found graphics books, blank storyboards and white copy paper in the drawers under the table. A waxing machine sat ready to work.

Leaving the study, Spencer closed the door. No one must suspect he had been here already. He ran up the stairs, two at a time. The cleaning crew had erased every trace of blood from the landing carpet, he noticed. Jersey's bedroom reminded him of a movie set, in black and gold. An arched doorway divided the narrow rectangle into two rooms. Another door led into a small closet and adjoining bathroom, but neither hid any secrets.

A sleigh bed, twin lacquered night chests and sculptured stone lamps furnished the sleeping area. Three silver-framed snapshots stood on a night chest, the only personal touches he could see. Spencer walked around the bed to take a closer look. One photograph was obviously Jersey's mother, the other her sister. The three women shared the same coloring, the shape of their jawbone. Mom had a streak of gray in her auburn curls; Sis was taller than Jersey. Spencer put the photographs back on the chest.

Where were the photos of Jenna, he wondered? He looked around him, realizing he hadn't seen any in Jersey's study, either. What proud mother kept no photos of her child?

He moved to the small sitting room fitted with a gold brocade chaise and a bookshelf full of bestsellers. Creases in the book spines told him they weren't for show. Spencer knelt to examine the bottom shelf, and found a clothbound photo album wedged above the other books. He levered it out, sat down on the chaise, already thumbing through it.

Pay dirt! Here was a whole album of Jenna. Her beautiful heart-shaped face framed with golden curls smiled up at him. He turned pages, memorizing her dimpled cheeks. Until now, he had nothing tangible to prove she even existed. Her green eyes, like matched gems, arrested him. In snapshot after snapshot, her mouth smiled, but her eyes did not. Suzanne Kirby's confirmation of sexual abuse smote him, breaking his heart. How could any man, much less her father, ruin such a beautiful child?

Could her mother have harmed her, as well, he wondered? He had to find this little girl, but where was she?

Realization dawned as he continued to study the album. Her clothes, her surroundings were from the late 1960's, not today. These photographs were not of Jenna, after all. They were of six-year-old Jersey. Frustration and anger clawed at his mind. He snapped the album shut and tucked it back in the bookcase. He closed the door to Jersey's room and walked to the other bedroom, hesitating before going in. What would he find inside, Spencer wondered?

The room was outfitted for a princess. Big pink roses swathed a canopy bed, matching the window shades. A white wicker cabinet was filled with everything a little girl could want. Tubs of Play-Doh, dancing music boxes, games and storybooks all looked well played with. Tropical fish darted in an aquarium. A large black teddy bear, in a plaid wool scarf, waited to pour tea at a child-sized table. Coloring books, crayons and water colors beckoned a child's imagination.

Spencer knelt to peek inside a dollhouse under large sunny windows. The jumbled rooms of furniture suggested it saw frequent play, as well. He stood and picked up a coloring book. Most of the pages were beautifully colored. Too perfectly done for a six-year-old, Spencer thought. He flipped through another book, all the pictures as neat as the first book. Either Jenna was a coloring prodigy, or Jersey did some coloring herself. Maybe it relieved stress, he thought, tossing the book on the table and opening another. These pages were not beautiful. These were smeared with black water paints. Rage and pain obliterated the tumbling kittens. He felt a familiar squeeze in his chest. Before he could stop it, a tear stained the page.

Friday, November 11

Part 35 of the San Diego County Criminal Court was alive with voices and bodies. A bailiff in crisp uniform called peoples to present themselves before Judge Georgeanne Morgan, a round-faced, black woman with salt and pepper hair, who finished one case and moved immediately to the next. Jersey waited in the small gallery, Cary Dodd at her side. Cary made top money defending his clients; his stride and attire reflected his status. She wore the dove-gray suit he had brought. She looked ready for a client meeting rather than a murder arraignment. Today was Cary's show; she only had one line. Jersey was ready. Cary was ready. Now, they waited for Judge Morgan to call their case.

Over her shoulder, Jersey saw Detective Phillips seated in back. His expression was unreadable, as bland as his umber suit. Few spectators were present, she noted. Two people took notes as each case finished. Jersey assumed them to be reporters. No cameras had flashed as she entered the court; no one shoved a microphone in her face. Jersey felt more than relieved; she was still anonymous.

"Calendar number seventeen," the bailiff sang out. "People versus Jersey Masters. Docket 024261, defendant charged with manslaughter in the first degree."

Jersey's attention snapped back to the proceedings. Cary entered the lawyer's arena. Ms. Regon, for the People of San Diego, looked young and smart in a slim black skirt and embroidered vest over a white silk blouse; her dark hair cut fashionably short. Judge Morgan rapped her gavel.

"At this time, I will ask the defendant to stand," the judge said. Jersey rose, looking stoical. "Miss Masters, you are charged with one count of voluntary manslaughter in the death of Daniel Miller. What is you plea?"

Jersey straightened her shoulders and met the judge's eyes. This all reminded her of a movie scene. "Am I guilty of murder?" She said. "No, I am not."

"Your Honor," Ms. Regon said. "The People request the defendant be bound over for trial with no bail."

"No bail?" Cary cut in, on cue. "My client is a respected member of her community with no prior record of any kind. She has a small child who does not deserve to be in the foster care system during the holidays."

"Counselor," Judge Morgan interrupted. "I don't see that the defendant's child is in the foster care system, at this time. Further, People notes the uncooperative nature of your client regarding her child's whereabouts."

"I am aware of my client's silence in this matter. I can assure the court, and the district attorney's office, that my client merely seeks to protect her child from repercussions surrounding her own actions."

"Is your client aware I can hold her in contempt of court, until such time as she produces the child?"

"She is, Your Honor," Cary said. "We would beg the court not to consider such a harsh penalty. My client assures me her child is in the care of relatives in Santa Cruz, California. I have no doubt of her veracity."

"The People have doubts, Your Honor." Ms. Regon said. "The little girl witnessed the events of Halloween night. We ask the court to grant temporary custody to the state, so we may ascertain what actually occurred between the defendant and the victim."

"The child is six," Cary argued. "Hardly a credible witness, Your Honor. We ask you to allow Miss Masters to visit her daughter and family during the holidays. Miss Masters will return with the child, and People may question her at that time, in her mother's presence."

"Your Honor, the People cannot agree. The nature of the crime, and the defendant's reluctance to cooperate, make her a flight risk."

"You make a compelling case, Ms. Regon," the judge said. "However, this court recognizes the defendant has no prior appearances before us. With a small child and strong community ties, the court believes she is a suitable candidate for bail, which I hereby set at five hundred thousand dollars, with a ten percent cash bond acceptable. Further, the court grants defense's request, allowing Miss Masters to spend the holiday with her family in Santa Cruz, California. Should the defendant not appear in my presence with the child, on Monday, November 28, I will swear out a warrant for her immediate arrest. A preliminary hearing is set for December one, nine a.m., part 49."

Judge Morgan banged her gavel. Jersey leapt to her feet. She felt like crowing, but held it in check. I'm free, she thought. Free to go home, free to get back to living! At least, for the next two weeks. Cary strode toward her. Jersey extended her hands, grasping his firmly, warmly. Her smile danced in her eyes.

"Thank you," she said.

"Not, yet," Cary said, but he smile. "Thank me once I've gotten your case dismissed. Or, when you're acquitted, whichever comes first."

Jersey waited as he handled the bail transaction then Cary escorted her from the courtroom, his hand hovering at her back. Jersey nodded, passing Detective Phillips. If he was happy for her, he didn't look it, she thought. She had probably spoiled his arrest record. If he wasn't happy, she didn't care.

In a narrow corridor with a low ceiling, Cary offered to drive her home, but Jersey declined. She watched him walk away, before making her way outside. Alone on the sidewalk, Jersey relished the normalcy of the afternoon. Hazy sunshine turned the sky golden. A soft breeze cooled her neck. Back East, folks looked forward to a crisp autumn Thanksgiving. In sunny San Diego, Jersey thought, the best they could hope for was some rain with their turkey. Two cabs parked at the taxi stand. She signaled, but neither driver saw her. Footsteps approached her from behind; she wheeled around.

"Detective Phillips." Her heart hammered, but her voice never faltered. "How nice to see you, again. Did you enjoy the performance?"

"May I offer you a ride home, Miss Masters?" He said, ignoring her barbs. "The cab drivers seem otherwise engaged."

"Thank you, no."

"It would only be fair. After all, I brought you to this dance."

"Very well," she said, smiling in spite of herself.

"That's the first time I've seen you smile. It doesn't look as bad on you as you think."

"What is it you want, detective?" Jersey bristled.

"To see you home, Miss Masters."

He smiled and cupped her elbow, leading her up the street. His Ford Taurus was parked in a nearby lot. Jersey waited for him to open the passenger door. Instinctively, Spencer safeguarded her head against striking the door as she slid into the seat. She adjusted her seatbelt as he rounded the back of the car. He climbed in and started the engine. Belted in, he joined the stream of traffic, going north. A laptop-sized computer between the seats created a barrier, matching their silence. Spencer drove, his eyes straight ahead. Jersey watched him in her peripheral vision. She felt no compunction to make small talk. Ten minutes later, he pulled into her driveway. As she stepped from the car, Spencer cleared his throat. Jersey hesitated, not turning.

"I was thinking," he said. "How would you feel about getting our kids together? Alison and Jenna have a lot in common, besides both being first graders."

"You're reaching, detective." She said, acidly. "Have a nice weekend."

Friday, November 11

Jersey bundled her mail from the box and let herself in, savoring the crisp gloom of her empty house. She wanted a long soak in a fragrant bath, but she needed to tend to a few things first. Jersey carried the mail into her study, kicking off her sandals. The brick tile felt cool and smooth under her bare feet. She tossed junk mail into a recycling bin, then rewound her answering machine. She had been away several days. Clients who hadn't read the papers would be wondering which corner of the earth she had fallen over. Those who had heard had probably called to cancel their business. Clients' voices spun out while she sat at her desk, making notes and locating files and phone numbers for return conversations.

"Hi, Jersey. 's Jenna." She listened as Jenna asked to come home, a playful smile teasing her lips. Good work, she thought. It would be great to get Jenna home, again. But, not yet. "I miss you, too, Honey Bunny," she whispered. "This will be over soon, I promise."

"Miss Masters, this is Brenda at Pacific Security. I'm notifying police that you've not responded to —"

"This is Detective Spencer Phillips with San Diego Police. We're already on the scene, Miss, uh, Brenda."

"What!" Jersey rewound the tape. " 'Miss Masters, this is Brenda at—,' " fast-forwarded. " '-Phillips with San Diego police—,' " forward again. " 'Could I have your badge number for our records?' " Jersey pressed her hands to her mouth, swallowing panic. He had been here! He had come here while she sat in jail. He had searched her house, looked for— Oh, God!

She flew to Jenna's room and threw open the door, gasping at the mess. Jenna's bed had been torn apart. Pillows and covers were heaped like leftover foliage pulled from a spring garden. Her drawers had been ransacked; someone had pawed through her games and books, dumping them on the floor. Fish floated in the aquarium, the stabilizing light unplugged. Jenna's dollhouse was in shambles. And, everywhere, that gritty black powder betrayed her.

God, oh god, oh god! Jersey stared around her, unbelieving. What to do, what to do? Her brain refused to help; rejected her need for assistance. She massaged her temples, hoping to recover function and reason. Where else had Phillips been? She quickly inventoried her own bedroom where everything seemed as she had left it. Except... her photograph album, had it protruded from the shelf like that before? What else did he know? Her machine had recorded his presence in her home early yesterday. Could Cary help her?

"I can't deal with this now," she moaned.

She headed for the bathroom. She had to calm down; she needed to decide what to do next. Jersey turned on the taps, full force, and added a generous squeeze of perfumed bubble bath. She caught her reflection in the mirror. So, this is what a jailbird looks like, she thought. Then, she chuckled, stripping off her clothes. She didn't look any different than she had two days ago. Let Detective Phillips search to his heart's content, she thought with a scoff. She had been right about him, after all. He didn't care about the circumstances of a matter. Why couldn't he just leave her alone, she wondered? His probing threatened her very existence, but she wouldn't let him win.

Jersey sank into the perfumed bubbles. The tub was large and oval, an extravagance she couldn't resist. She had had to break into Jenna's closet to make room for it, but it had been worth it. Jenna called it their swimming pool, since the backyard wasn't big enough for one. Jersey smiled, remembering the mess of making this house their home. Tearing out old flooring, bringing in authentic Mexican tiles for the downstairs floors and the kitchen counters, scouring Mexican boutiques for pottery and knickknacks. She sighed with contentment, the warm water reaching into her muscles and the musty-smelling suds soothing her thoughts.

Her life was too quiet without Jenna's constant chatter. Could she stand it until Jenna came home? Jersey missed the little girl's companionship. Friday nights were Jenna's nights. Whatever she wanted to do, they did. Usually, Jenna chose pizza, popcorn and videos. Sometimes, they took burgers to a drive-in theater.

On the other hand, Jersey thought. Without Jenna here, she had had no nightmares, a welcome relief. She eased deeper into the hot water. Tomorrow, she had a fundraising dinner to attend, and then a trade show for franchise owners on Sunday. Trade shows were great business opportunities for her. With a pocketful of business cards and a head full of good ideas, she could easily walk away with half-a-dozen new clients.

Across the street, Spencer adjusted his seat to a reclining position, watching Jersey's house. He had draped his jacket and tie over the passenger seat, settling in for the night. He had intended to head home after dropping her off. Instead, he had parked at the opposite curb, watching her move about her study. When she suddenly leapt up and dashed from the room, he decided his laundry could wait. When pizza arrived later, Spencer ordered a return trip.

An hour later, her house was dark save for a tiny light glimmering through Jersey's bedroom window. His car smelled of Italian herbs and congealing cheese. He wore his earphones, playing the two tapes of Jenna back to back, over and over. He knew every word by heart; knew each turn of her voice, its cadences and rhythms a part of his soul now.

Guilt licked his intestines; his clandestine search of Jersey's home disturbed him. He had never so blatantly disregarded his authority. Was it more than frustration, he wondered? Police didn't care why crimes were committed, he reminded himself. Police arrested suspects and turned over evidence to those whose job it was to care.

He had to admit he was damn glad Jersey had made bail. She had killed Daniel Miller for molesting Jenna, and part of him cheered. He gladly would have killed the bastard who raped his niece. As a cop, he didn't have that luxury. He believed in justice, not vigilante-ism. But, he was fast becoming disillusioned with a system that saw only black and white; a system that arrested a woman for defending her child from a molester, while he walked away without a thought to the damage that he had done.

Parents who put their children in jeopardy infuriated him. He had no Savior complex, Spencer knew; just eleven years as a peace officer. He had seen children hit by cars and people. He had rescued children from sewer drains, and their own sense of invincibility. He always kept his cool, if not his heart. Well, almost always, he thought, remembering a three-year-old drug bust. Dear old dad had fed his bouncing baby boy cocaine-filled balloons to smuggle it across the Mexican border. The baby died when a balloon ruptured. Spencer had nearly beaten that father to a pulp.

Spencer hit Rewind, then Play. " '-he didn't s'posed to come here,' " Jenna sobbed. " 'Jersey didn't say he could come here, but he just did. But, he didn't s'posed to and...and I did kill him with that gun.' "

"Jenna, do you live at 418 Presidio Crest Drive?"

"Uh huh, 's Jersey's house."

He stopped the tape. "Jersey's house?" Jenna hadn't said "my house" or "Mommy's house." Why hadn't he caught that before? He looked at the sleeping house, puzzled. He traded the 911 tape for the copy of Jenna's message to - Jersey! Some parents, he knew, were on a first-name basis with their children. Some parents struggled with their own lost youth, preferring to raise their best friends, rather than their children. Jersey Masters didn't strike him as such a mother.

What type of mother did Jersey strike him as, he wondered? Any mom who furnished her daughter with the bedroom Jenna had either really loved her daughter, or really loved the status it bought. Jersey kept chocolate ice cream in her freezer, and she took time to color with her child. At the same time, she taught Jenna to pick up after herself. No small feat, he thought, considering his niece and nephew. Of course, he had never seen Jersey interact with her daughter, Spencer realized. And, Jersey hid from the world, which ruled her out as a prestige hound. He had to admit he was physically attracted to Jersey, though he didn't trust her. Her outer calm raised too many suspicions.

Jenna's similarities to Alison drew him into this case unlike any since that drug bust. If he was honest with himself, he was more attracted to the child than to her mother. He wanted to protect Jenna in the way her father should have. He wanted to make her safe - to see her smile, just once. He couldn't let go of this case until he had made sure Jenna was okay. Once he found her, could he help Jenna feel safe? Alison's single episode had left her traumatized. What must Jenna feel, abused and abandoned by her own father?

He needed answers. Spencer cupped his face in his hands, breathing stale pepperoni air. A name popped into his brain: Dr. Kaneally, Alison's psychologist. She could give him answers.

Some time later, the sun woke him. Spencer sat up, running his hands through his copper hair, rubbing himself awake. Jersey's Mustang was still in her driveway, he noted with satisfaction. He switched on the car radio. A disk jockey announced it was seven-thirty on a clear crisp November morning. His stomach demanded food; were there any crusts left from last night? He tossed the empty pizza box into the back seat and started the car. Breakfast first, then home to shower and tackle those perpetual housekeeping tasks. His suit would need a trip through the dry cleaners, after treating it like pajamas. He tucked his portable player into his coat pocket, keeping Jenna near at hand. He would call Alison, too. She deserved a special date with Uncle Spencer.

Monday, November 14

Spencer entered the squad room at nine a.m. Lucky, he thought, considering morning traffic on I-5. He meant to phone Dr. Kaneally first thing.

"Good morning, Detective." Bonnie, the P.A.A. greeted him with a handful of messages. "How was your weekend?"

"Great! Alison's T-ball team won their first game."

Doffing his blue blazer, he slung it over his chair, reaching for his telephone. Mateo rushed at him, carrying a two-foot high stack of files. Spencer deliberately turned his back. Mateo dropped the files on his desk.

"Spence, how'd you like me to fix you up with this gorgeous blond actress I know?"

Spencer faced his partner, holding out the receiver. "Apparently you've not seen this activity before. I'm making a telephone call here. I'm attempting to connect with another human being who is also familiar with this process."

"Her name is Laurel Sweeten. I met her at the club pool, yesterday."

"Not interested, Mateo." He turned his back, again.

"I'm telling you, man. She's perfect for you. Tall, skinny, big blue eyes. She had on this turquoise bikini." He emphasized its skimpiness with gestures. "No guy there could stand up straight, if you catch me."

"I do, Rivera," Spencer said. "But, if she's so perfect, why don't you date her?"

"I said she's perfect for you. My Mama would drop dead if I took up with some blond gringa."

"Your family's still living in the Dark Ages, huh?"

"Is that a pun?" Mateo asked, inspecting his forearm. They laughed. "Seriously, let me do this for you. I told her about you, and she's interested in meeting you. Laurel is gorgeous. Or, don't you go for that type?"

All right, all right." Spencer surrendered. "Set it up. How bad can she be?"

"You won't regret it," Mateo said.

"Let me rephrase. She better not be bad, or you will regret it."

Rivera left the files on his desk. Spencer referred to a business card and punched in the phone number. Dr. Kaneally's phone rang eight times, then a woman asked him to hold a moment. He cupped his mouth, then reached for his coffee. He sipped and grimaced; it tasted cold and astringent, leftover from last night he realized. He waited, silence buzzing in his ear.

"Hello," she said, at last. "This is Dr. Kaneally. How can I help you?"

"Doctor; Detective Spencer Phillips. Alison Thurber's uncle."

"Oh yes, detective. Alison mentions you often."

"I need some information on early sexual trauma. The better informed I am, the better I can do my job. And, I want to better understand what my niece is going through."

"This doesn't sound like something we can do over the phone."

"I'd prefer not to. I have a lot of questions."

Spencer heard her turning pages. "I have an hour, Friday morning at eleven," she said. "If that fits your schedule?"

"Friday at eleven is fine. Thank you, Doctor."

"Hey, Spence." Rivera called. He also had a phone growing from his ear. "Laurel says she can meet you for lunch on Friday, okay?"

"Sure," he called back, waving absently. He began listing his questions for Dr. Kaneally.

"Hotel Internationale, one o'clock. Look for a beautiful blond in a red dress."

"I'll be there," he murmured.

Thursday, November 17

The Carlsbad High School Lancers rode out to meet their opponents on the field of green, armored in royal purple and gold, eager for the game to begin. Their ladies cheered them from the sideline, fair damsels waving them on with their frothy pompoms. Spencer, with Alison on his shoulders, joined the spectators on their feet as the adversaries squared off and the football was thrust into play. At his side, Belinda captured the duel on video, training the mechanical eye on number 36. Scott, Jr., a valiant knight of the backfield, quickly pierced the opposing black-and-red defense and scored the first touchdown, his family screaming with enthusiasm. Then, the freshman soldiers mounted their defense, holding back the foe as it pushed toward the goal line.

By halftime, the Lancers led 14 to 6. Alison was asleep on her uncle's lap; her head nestled into the hollow of Spencer's shoulder. Alison looked like her dad with her Liz Taylor blue eyes and flaxen mop of curls. Scott, Jr. had inherited the Phillips' coloring - strawberry blonde hair and plenty of freckles. Spencer cupped Alison's cheek, firm and warm as a sun-ripened peach, and desire swamped him. He marveled at the devotion he felt for his niece. How much stronger would his feelings be for his own child? Then, he realized how thin was the veil between civility and depravity; perhaps, indistinguishable to a man like Daniel Miller. But, Spencer's feelings prompted him to shield and protect this little girl. What prompted a man to act on carnal passions?

Perhaps, Dr. Kaneally could provide an answer, Spencer

thought, adding the question to his mental notebook. For the last two days, he had brooded through his work. He had so many unanswered questions, felt so many conflicted feelings. What drove him to illegally search Jersey's house? What caused him to sleep in his car at her curb rather than risk missing a glimpse of Jenna? He felt guilty about invading Jersey's home, and disturbed that he had lost his objectivity, in total disregard for the law. He was frustrated and - if he had to admit it - panicked that he hadn't found Jenna. And, on top of everything else, Mateo had roped him into a blind date where he was now required to be charming and engaging, when all he wanted to do was find one six-year-old girl.

"You're preoccupied, tonight," Belinda said, setting a tray of sodas from the concession stand between them. "You haven't heckled a referee, all night."

"Yeah." He nodded.

"Is it a case? Anything you can tell me about?"

"Another little girl, probably molested by her father. Now, he's dead at the hands of her mother and I'm supposed to treat the woman like she's any other criminal, as if she's the villain."

"No way to let the mom go?"

"She's already scheduled for a preliminary hearing."

"It's more than what happened to Alison, isn't it, Spence?"

She knew him too well, he thought. "Yeah," he said, again.

"I'm sorry." She rested her hand on his shoulder.

"God, Belinda!" He cupped his face in his free hand. "I'm getting so sick of it all. I'm fed up with selfish, unfeeling adults using their children."

"And, you're reluctant to become another selfish, unfeeling adult?"

"Exactly. Putting that woman in jail could have meant subjecting that little girl to further abuse. Instead, I've got a mother in jail facing possible contempt charges because she won't give up her child's whereabouts. It's the perverts who deserve to be punished, not the victims."

"You're not an unfeeling adult, Spencer. You're just doing your job." Belinda stroked his arm.

"I don't know how long I can keep doing it." He pictured himself rummaging through Jersey's freezer for body parts, and sighed. "Eleven years have jaded me. When we were growing up, I never looked at my classmates wondering whose parents were brutalizing them."

"Of course not. We were just kids."

"Now, every child I see, I wonder - are they safe? Are they still innocent? Are the people who are supposed to nurture them, in fact torturing them?" Spencer looked down at the sleeping child cradled against his chest. "You can't trust the village, any more. The people in it are too sick."

"I don't believe that!" Belinda said. "I can't believe that and I won't raise my children to believe that. I have to believe most people are like us. Living their lives and doing the best they can to keep the scary parts away from all our kids."

"But, what do you do when it isn't enough?" He asked, still looking at Alison.

"Well, I know you. You're a good detective - you're a good man. That's what makes you a good detective. When you want something bad enough, you get it. This woman couldn't ask for a better champion."

The teams took the field again, fortified to continue the match. The purple-and-gold cheerleaders began rallying the crowd to its feet for the second-half kickoff. Belinda jumped to her feet and aimed her camera, leaving Spencer with his niece and his recitations of guilt and frustration.

Friday, November 18

Dr. Kaneally's office was on the fourth floor of a brick and glass building in Mission Valley. Spencer took Waring Road, turned right at the stoplight, and then proceeded down a gentle slope to the commercial complex. Its windows looked black, reflecting the morning sun onto the green and brown hills across the freeway. Exhaust fumes from the steady drone of traffic above spoiled the country atmosphere.

Spencer parked in a visitor's space. He looked sharp, dressed in his navy worsted over gray flannel slacks and black loafers, in honor of his date later. A short flight of steps brought him into a narrow lobby and to a set of bronze-colored elevator doors. A lone banana palm struggled to dispel the lifelessness of the room. He rehearsed his questions on the ride up. When he stepped out, Dr. Kaneally waved at him from the end of the corridor.

"I'm between receptionists, at the moment," she explained, gripping his hand. "The employment agency downstairs ran an ad for me. Now, I have fifty-two applicants to interview."

She looked like a typical California girl, Spencer thought. Sun-burnished skin and a buxom body under a taupe linen suit. Her dark blond ponytail hung down her back. Tiny laugh lines hinted at her age. She had a line of silver hoops running up her left ear.

Natural colors and textures decorated her office. He looked around the room. A slab of monkey pod on chrome sawhorses served as her desk. Bookshelves lined one wall, stacked with children's books and games. Her credentials hung next to a large photograph of orange and white sailboats on North San Diego Bay. Spencer recognized the spot; he and his father had sailed there, often.

"I took it myself," she said, noticing his interest.

"You're very good."

"I photograph beautiful scenery to forget the ugliness of my work."

"Maybe I should try that," he said, remembering why he was here.

An art caddy sat in the middle of a large round table surrounded by blue canvas director's chairs. He knelt to peer into the tidy rooms of a dollhouse, reminded of the one in Jenna's bedroom.

"It serves a dual purpose," Dr. Kaneally said. "Some children can only deal with their trauma through play. I can't tell you how many daddies I've replaced."

This daddy had black hair, a painted on tie and glasses, and Daniel Miller came to his mind. "I can imagine," he said.

"In your line of work, I'm sure you can." She sat down at the table, resting her forearms on it. "You said you had questions?"

He sat, also. "Doctor —"

"Call me Judith, please."

"Judith, I want to understand what happened - what is happening - to my niece; the dynamics of sexual molestation. What happens, psychologically, to a child who's abused? And, what are the long-term effects?"

"I understand your concerns for you niece," Judith said. "I assure you, Alison is doing very well. I don't foresee any long-term effects. Once our work is through, she should lead a perfectly normal life."

"Speaking in general, what does your work entail?"

"Basically, I teach children to deal with their feelings. Children have so little power over their own worlds. Abuse robs them of the security they've come to depend on. They can't feel safe, any more. A child feels tremendous rage, over this loss. We learn to channel that rage into appropriate responses. And, to put the blame for the loss on the appropriate party, namely the abuser.

"Children who aren't allowed to be angry, can turn their rage onto others, becoming abusers themselves. Or, they turn it inward, resulting in self-destructive behaviors such as substance abuse or self-mutilation. I'm sure you're familiar with the patterns."

Spencer nodded. "I've been trained to spot abuse. It didn't prepare me to deal with it in my own family, however."

"I don't think anything can prepare you for that," Judith said. "Children like Alison, who are assaulted only once, recover much quicker. A supportive family helps them feel safer, sooner."

"What about the child, sexually abused by a family member, who has no support?" Spencer cupped his face, thinking of Jenna.

"Naturally, prolonged abuse of any kind has devastating effects. Abuse by a family member is the ultimate betrayal. Studies show a child who is sexually abused by her father experiences death, if you will, a death of her spirit. It's as if the parent murders his child. Recovery, if there is such a thing, is a slow process. I mean, a child who cannot trust her parent to keep her world safe, feels she can't trust anyone."

"Are you using female pronouns on purpose?"

"Sorry, color me politically incorrect. Most molest victims are girls, but the devastation is just as great for boys. Rebuilding trust is the hardest work we do. Often, children repress those painful times, and fight against reliving them."

"How can a child repress that kind of trauma?"

Judith folded her arms across her chest. "It's not a simple process, by any means," she said. "It's a matter of survival. But, denying the abuse takes its own toll on the psyche. Dissociative disorders, for example."

"Multiple personalities?" He asked, skeptical "Have you experienced this firsthand?"

"Not firsthand, no. Textbook MPD, however, occurs when a very young child experiences severe, repeated abuse. The younger the child, the greater risk of splitting the personality. The child creates other persons, if you will, who handle the abuse. Each personality assumes a role. Some are aware of the others, some are not."

"So, severely abused children cope by making up other people. Is that what you're saying?"

"That's a simplification, but yes." Judith nodded. "It's not a conscious process, by any means. A child most often doesn't realize she's done this. Children see themselves, and others, as good and bad. They don't know how to see the gray areas of life, yet. And, sexual abuse causes them tremendous guilt. 'What did I do to deserve this?' "

"They feel like they're being punished," he offered. "But, they don't know why."

She nodded, again. "So, they cope by letting the abuse happen to the bad person. Then, they separate themselves from that bad person."

"I have to say, Doctor - Judith. I find this multiple personality stuff hard to believe. Every scumbag out there blames his crimes on his lousy childhood. And, how about the current rash of false memories implanted by overzealous shrinks? How can I believe anyone who claims they were abused?"

"I have a book that might be very helpful," Judith said.

Friday, November 18

Spencer sped over the five-and-a-quarter miles of freeway into downtown San Diego. His interview with Alison's doctor had taken longer than planned; now he was late for his lunch date. He verified the time on his wrist; lunch-hour traffic could be horrendous, especially on a Friday. He could spend the next half-hour eating exhaust.

Butterflies tumbled in his gut as he anticipated meeting Mateo's friend. Spencer had never married, though he had come close twice. A college romance ended when he and she discovered they wanted different things in life. Then, three years ago, his second fiancée realized she couldn't handle the stress of being engaged to a police officer and broke it off. He didn't date, as a rule, preferring to spend his off-duty hours with his sister and her kids. Belinda was older, but Spencer had always thought of himself as her big brother. It surprised him how close they were now, they hadn't been growing up. He had enjoyed boating, hiking in the deserts, and surfing. Belinda liked writing poems; often spending days locked in her room, scribbling in a notebook. She had written her first one at age seven, and published it in the local newspaper. He had never understood her, then. She now worked in the offices at Arco arena.

It was just the two of them, now. Their father had worked forty-five years as a typesetter for the San Diego Union, before it merged with its rival newspaper, The Tribune. Mom had taught junior and senior English at Kearney Mesa High School. When she died of breast cancer in 1990, Pop retired to his family home in Greenwich, Connecticut. He and his brother now owned a print shop.

Belinda had married her high school sweetheart Scott Thurber right after graduation, and Scott Jr. was born thirteen months later. Scott was a police officer in Miramar, until he was killed six years ago, during what should have been a routine traffic stop. After Scott's death, Belinda moved to Carlsbad, as far away from San Diego as she could get without leaving behind her brother, her sole familial support. Within a month of the funeral, Belinda discovered she was pregnant, so Spencer coached her through labor. His beautiful niece had seen his face, even before her mother's. Spencer smiled at the fond memory.

Spencer parked his sedan in the hotel basement and rode the elevator to the marble and sparkle lobby. He searched the dining room for a tall blond in a red suit, whose figure had stopped men in their tracks last week. Over the crowd, such a woman waved. Mateo hadn't exaggerated, he thought. Laurel Sweeten had a wholesome Midwestern beauty. Spencer threaded his way around tables where business deals worth more than his annual salary were discussed over meals that would set him back a day's pay. Already, he knew Ms. Sweeten was too rich for his blood, if this was her usual hangout.

Near the center of the room, a familiar voice distracted him. There, Jersey Masters entertained an executive Spencer recognized from the newspapers. He hadn't seen her since the arraignment. She looked stunning in a tailored black suit, her bronze curls swept into a tortoiseshell clip. She spoke animatedly, punctuating her sentences with one hand. The two shared a pitcher of Bloody Mary's and an antipasto platter. Spencer slowed his pace, studying her.

"I understand your reservations, Stewart," she said. "A speech expresses your personality, as well as the subject matter. You've seen my work on a very successful mayoral campaign. Now, you just have to let me work that same magic for you."

She looked up, saw him approaching. She sat back in her chair and laid her hands in her lap, bringing down a curtain of civility.

"Good afternoon, Miss Masters." Spencer said, smiling. "A pleasant surprise."

"A happy coincidence?" She replied, tartly.

"I'm meeting a friend," he said, indicating the blond half a room away

"You do very well on a police officer's salary."

"Oh, are you a police officer?" Her companion gushed.

"Detective Spencer Phillips, homicide." He extended his hand, guessing the man's exuberant curiosity resulted from the Bloody Mary's.

"Homicide? How intriguing. Jersey, whom did you murder?"

"I murdered no one, Stewart," she said, smoothly. "Detective Phillips and I are professional acquaintances."

Spencer admired her cool. Most cops experienced an emotional meltdown after their first shooting; he had thrown up for a week. Jersey Masters appeared unscathed by her first killing. Perhaps, it hadn't been her last, he thought with ire.

"By the way, Miss Masters, is your daughter home-schooled?"

"I didn't know you had a daughter," Stewart said.

"I think your guest is growing impatient, detective," Jersey said.

"Yes, well. I should go. I'll be in touch soon."

"Somehow, I knew you would be." Her smile bit him.

Laurel stood, as he approached, and extended both hands. Spencer took her hands in his and she leaned into him, smelling expensive, kissing the air beside his cheek as if they were dearest friends. Then, she wiped away imaginary lipstick traces with red-tipped fingers.

"Red looks much better on me," she teased. Her throaty voice held a residue of Midwestern twang.

"It's nice to meet you," he said.

"I was beginning to think you'd had a better offer." She nodded in Jersey's direction.

"Business."

"Really?" She leaned in, whispering, "Which one is the criminal?"

Spencer seated himself, his back to Jersey Masters. He would have preferred to face her, but Laurel was already sitting there and he couldn't think how to change seats without arousing her suspicion. A waiter materialized, as they sat down. Because he was still on duty, Spencer ordered club soda. Laurel already had white wine. They studied their menus, Laurel chatting amiably behind hers. Spencer heard little of what she said, his attention straining toward the other table. When the waiter returned, he ordered a Caesar salad, the least expensive item he could find. Laurel ordered broiled chicken sans skin, fat and taste. The waiter took their menus before he disappeared.

"Mateo tells me you're an actress," he said, looking her for the first time. "Would I have seen you in anything?"

"Not unless you're into feminine hygiene products." She laughed, lightly. "Actually, I'm an administrative assistant for a mortgage broker firm. Though, I did have a small part on NYPD Blue, last year. I played a corpse in a Dumpster."

He nodded, wondering if Jersey was still behind him. He couldn't hear her voice anymore. He couldn't see the door, either. Gratefully, their lunches arrived and he could concentrate on eating without seeming rude.

"Mateo tells me you played baseball in college." She nibbled a nude broccoli floweret. "You're so tall, I'd have guessed you played basketball."

"Too cliché," he said.

"Were you any good? Did you have aspirations?" She asked, making aspirations sound naughty.

Spencer ignored her tone. "I broke my femur, my second season, sliding into third base. My coach said my height and weight were a liability. My aspirations ended there."

"Ouch!" She pouted prettily and reached across the table, but didn't touch him.

Why had Mateo thought he would like her, Spencer wondered? Laurel was always auditioning. At one thirty he escorted her to her car, a red Miata. Jersey's midnight blue Mustang was nowhere, though he hadn't noticed it on the way in either, he thought. As he held Laurel's door, she cupped his cheek and kissed his ear, making actual contact this time. This time, she didn't wipe away the lipstick.

"I hope we'll do this again," she said, thrusting forth her chin.

"I enjoyed lunch," he said, closing her door. "But, I don't think we'll do it again."

Sunday, November 20

Jersey plunged into darkness, again and ran for her life. She didn't know where she was going and she couldn't see anything. Why did this keep happening? Any minute, she could catapult into a wall or trip over some unseen obstacle, but she had to keep running. Her own labored breathing pierced the silence. Her lungs begged to stop, please! Terror urged her on. Run, run! Keep running! She had to get away from - what? There! Footsteps chased her; heavy footfalls closed in on her. Who was it? The same someone who had hovered just out of reach? Jersey didn't want to find out. She ran faster. So did the footsteps behind her, coming quicker and closer and she realized she couldn't outrun them.

"Is he comin, yet, Jersey?" Jenna wailed.

Where was Jenna? Jersey tried to search around her, but it was too dark. Where are you, Honey Bunny? Her lungs threatened to burst if she didn't stop running, but she didn't dare. Oh god, oh god! She had to stop. She had to —!

Jersey struggled up, gulping air. Was she followed? Had Jenna escaped? She looked around; sunlight poured into her bedroom. Her room! She was home, safe. She laughed with relief, and then she flung off her covers and ran into her closet. She yanked on leggings and a huge sweater, stomped into a pair of running shoes. She pounded down the stairs, threw back the locks and ran out of the house, ignoring the pot of rich scented coffee brewing in the kitchen.

She ran toward Heritage Park and the San Diego Mission. She

ran smoothly, without thought. The November sky was blue, the air tasted crisp and sweet. She filled her lungs with it, dispelling the terror with each exhale. Someone was frying bacon. The old mission bells welcomed the new day with happy peals. Jersey ran toward them, grateful for the sound and the sunlight. Her shoes slapped the asphalt, harmonizing with the bells. In the park, she slowed to a walk, leaving the gravel paths to wander over verdant slopes. Tourists were already snapping photos and marveling at the bronze markers that commemorated the founding fathers of one of California's first missions. Jersey wove her way through the visitors, tunneled into her own thoughts.

Why was she having nightmares? At last, she allowed herself to think. Why were the dreams back? And, why couldn't she shut them out? The dreams had started Halloween night. Daniel Miller's legacy? Jersey cursed him again. The dreams had a recurring theme, she realized. Darkness, a dangerous presence that pursued her, and a small frightened child. Obviously, the child was Jenna, she thought. But, who stalked her?

What if they weren't dreams? What if they were memories? The sudden thought chilled her, and Jersey shivered. How could she find out, she wondered. Maybe, Jenna remembered her father. She had never asked the child what she remembered, she had never thought to ask. If Jenna remembered, Jersey thought, maybe she could learn how to turn off the nightmares. She would have to wait to find out, though. Once she and Jenna came together in Santa Cruz, she would ask, Jersey decided. She couldn't risk bringing Jenna back until she was safe from the ever-vigilant Detective Phillips.

It was as if Phillips was stalking her. She glanced around now, expecting to see him jog up behind her. He wasn't leaning against a tree either, waiting for her to catch up. Her chest tightened, and she took several cleansing breaths. What could he do if he found Jenna, she wondered? He couldn't take her away, certainly. But, he could cause problems at the hearing, problems that would keep them apart for a long time.

No! Anger plumbed her depths. She wouldn't let him do that. Jenna was her child, she always would be. And, Jenna had memories that would stop the nightmares, Jersey felt sure. Everything would return to normal, once she knew the key. Jersey shook out her hair, and picked up her pace. She was not powerless! She had control of the situation and her life. She circled the rose gardens, once more, and headed for home.

Wednesday, November 23

Spencer sat at his desk in shirtsleeves, attempting to move his "in" basket to his "out" basket. Two hours remained in his shift, he could feasibly empty both trays, he thought. He was working the swing shift again. Tomorrow was Thanksgiving and he had four days off. Though it was early morning, phones rang and other detectives talked, worked and drank coffee. A cleaning crew emptied wastebaskets and vacuumed up non-human debris. Since dusk yesterday, there had been one hit and run, four break-ins and a stabbing in Balboa Park. Darkness tended to bolster the courage of otherwise law-abiding citizens, he thought, closing another case file.

Four days off, he thought, cupping his face in his hands. The last time he had a four-day Thanksgiving vacation, he was a college student. He opened the next report, an attempted rape the accused's lawyer pleaded out. Crime cost so little these days, a true bargain for any perp. Jenna's voice filtered into his consciousness. He touched his recorder. He didn't need to play it to hear her, any more.

"Hey, Spence." Rivera waved his hand in front of his eyes.

He looked up. Mateo wore a slate-gray suit and blue shirt. "Sorry?"

"Don't worry about it. Paperwork often inspires daydreaming in me, too. How was your date with Laurel?"

"We weren't soul mates, after all."

"Too bad. Maybe next time. I hear you've got four days off.

Going to your sister's?"

"Belinda's expecting me in Carlsbad, at nine tomorrow morning. How 'bout you?"

"Me?" Rivera pointed to his chest. "I'm a working stiff, remember? I'll be eating my turkey at the local Denny's."

"Sorry to hear that. What can I do for you today, Mateo?"

"It's what you asked me to do for you. I've searched birth records in San Diego, Santa Cruz, LA and San Francisco. Jenna Miller has no birth certificate in any city; neither does Jenna Masters. We went back four to eight years, nothing anywhere."

Spencer sat back, mentally munching. "So, Jersey had her baby somewhere else."

"Or, she never had a baby, at all."

"Both Suzanne Kirby and Miller's widow say she did."

"I still say the woman's a fruitcake. What do you want me to do, now?"

"I'm not sure," Spencer said. His phone rang, but he ignored it. "Let me take the weekend to decide."

"You got it. Happy Thanksgiving, Spence."

"You too, Mateo." Spencer's phone kept ringing. He yanked the receiver from its cradle and barked into it.

"Happy holiday to you, too," Nancy Addison said.

"Don't pay any attention to me. That's just my foot-in-mouth disease acting up, again."

"A chronic case?"

"Incurable, I'm afraid." He chuckled. "You got the match on Jenna Miller?"

"That's why I called. Not a single print belongs to a little girl."

"No mistake? You're positive?"

"As positive as I can be," Nancy said. "Every print you brought me belongs to Jersey Masters."

"Okay, thanks all the same."

Spencer cupped his face in his hands. How did a little girl live in a house and leave no trace of herself? Jersey was a thorough housekeeper; perhaps she cleaned after taking Jenna to Santa Cruz, wiping away Jenna's presence. But, when had she taken Jenna to Santa Cruz, he thought with a start. He had placed an officer at her door, that first night. If Jersey had gone out, he would have known. She could have put the child on a plane before they arrived; no one had seen Jenna that night. He shook his head, the timing was wrong. She couldn't have gotten Jenna out so quickly. So, where was she?

Maybe Mateo was right about Jersey Masters. He shoved the thought away, pushing away the rape file. Damn! Jersey Masters was a cool head. Did anything rattle that woman? He fingered his cassette player wondering what to try next.

Supposing he told Jersey he had spoken to her daughter, had called her in Santa Cruz and Jenna told him all about the shooting? Would that shake Jersey's resolve? Either she would laugh in his face, knowing he couldn't have talked to her because Jenna was dead, or she would break into a tearful confession. Jersey Masters breaking into tears? He scoffed at the thought. More likely, she would become enraged. And, in the heat of anger, the truth might come out. He snatched his brown jacket from the back of his chair and sprinted for his car.

Spencer parked across the street from Jersey's home. The midmorning sky was white as ice. He took several deep breaths, gripping and releasing the steering wheel. His brain was a mess of unanswered questions and disbelief. He had to play it casual, he told himself. Masters became defensive whenever Jenna's whereabouts were questioned. He opened his door and stepped out. Jersey opened her front door, at the same moment, and came out carrying a suitcase and overnight bag. She wore pale denims, boots and a brown bomber jacket. Her auburn curls fell loose around her shoulders. Spencer leaned against his car, watching her put her bags in her trunk. Then, she got in her car and drove away.

He should have stopped her, he knew. She was going to her mother's with the court's blessings, no less. At the very least, he should have confronted her, especially in light of Nancy's find-

ings. But, he had stood and watched her go, caught off-guard by -
what? What had stopped him?

Jenna. A heavy disappointment weighed on him. He realized
how much he looked forward to seeing the little girl he carried in
his pocket. Had Jersey told the truth, or was Mateo right in his
suspicions? Did Jenna exist, or didn't she? Was her voice on a tape
enough to convince him she lived? Could he rely on the word of a
neighbor and a widow? He could follow Jersey to Santa Cruz, and
alienate his family in the process. Short of that, he had to wait for
her to return. He would be right here, when she did.

Wednesday, November 23

Jersey switched on the heater, settled back in her seat and adjusted her seat belt. Santa Cruz was an hour away. North of San Clemente, she had switched to the Pacific Coast Highway, a longer more beautiful route, with the silver-blue ocean on her left and strings of tiny beachfront towns on the right. All day, a high fog had lingered near the shore, like a new suitor reluctant to see the date end. She drove with the top down, tasting salt air until the sun set, taking its warmth with it. The night sky hung over her, painted with purple clouds and white stars. The surf crashed outside. Inside, Harry Connick, Jr. crooned from the radio.

A familiar longing tugged at her when Jersey thought of seeing her mother and sister again. It was a longing tinged with loneliness. Going home reminded her she was the outsider. Mom and Patrice shared something she could never be a part of. Maybe, it was because Patrice had married and settled near their mother, while she had moved eight hundred miles away. But, Jersey had felt this way long before moving to San Diego. Was it the loneliness or the longing to be a part of her own family that pulled her back each year?

"Are we almost there, yet, Jersey?"

"Well hi, Honey Bunny." She glanced at the sleeping girl and smiled. The dash lights illuminated her sweet face. "You're awake."

"Mm hmm." Jenna yawned.

"We're almost there, I promise. Do you need to stop for the restroom?"

"No." She yawned again, resting her head against the door, watching out her window.

"What are you looking at, Honey Bunny."

"I like to look at the diamonds on the street."

"Diamonds?"

"Mm hmm. See?" Jenna pointed.

Jersey looked and saw tiny bits of light, glittering in her headlamps. "Oh, diamonds," she said. "Unfortunately, those diamonds were left by an accident, or someone throwing away a drink bottle."

"I know. I just like to think they're diamonds."

Jenna's idealism tore at her heart. Watching the road, Jersey tried to think of a time when she had seen diamonds in bits of broken glass. She shook her head; conjuring up that kind of innocence was beyond her. Caution and skepticism had dogged her as long as she could remember.

"How about we stop for some French fries and a milkshake?"

"Mm hmm!" Jenna's eyes sparkled like diamonds. "I'm glad we're not playing hide-and-seek now, Jersey."

"Me too, Honey Bunny." She smiled and pushed away her thoughts.

* * * * *

The clock on her dash read eight-thirty when Jersey turned into her mother's driveway. She parked behind her mom's old Volvo in the gravel drive and sat back, struck again by the sameness of it all. The old house never changed or aged, Jersey thought. The large two-story house with white clapboard siding couched behind a brick and picket fence; the rosebushes, now winter-bare, standing sentinel at the front door. She had grown up in this house; it would always feel like home. Jersey got her bags from her trunk and headed for the back door. Mom always kept the front one locked. She reminded Jenna to stay right behind her, and went inside.

"Hi! Anyone home?" Jersey called, letting the screen door thump her hip.

"In here," they answered together.

She set her suitcases beside the washing machine and went into the kitchen. The air smelled redolent with sweet and spicy pumpkin pies. Patrice stood beside their mother at the butcher-block island. They each had a paring knife, dicing onions and celery for stuffing. Both wore a dishtowel tucked into their waistbands. The dishwasher hummed, underscoring their task. Mom wiped her hands on her towel as she came around to hug Jersey. She wore white nursing slacks and a maroon Dominican Santa Cruz Hospital tee shirt. Her still-auburn hair sported a white streak in her bangs.

"How've you been, honey?"

"Fine, Mom. You? How're things at the hospital?"

The dishwasher finished and Mom went to turn it off. Jersey shrugged, she would ask again later. Patrice mimicked her mother, wiping her hands on her towel and coming to hug her. She was several inches shorter than Jersey; her light red hair hung in sheets from a center part, her blue eyes smiled into Jersey's.

"How's work?" Patrice said.

"Going well. How are your boys?"

"Oh, real good. Ben is junior class president, and Gabe took third place at this year's speech decathlon. Ward will bring them in the morning. Tonight, they're doing some father-son bonding."

Mom and Patrice resumed chopping vegetables.

"What can I do to help?" Jersey asked.

"Oh, honey," Mom said. "Just stand back and let us work. You don't get much chance to cook living alone, I'm sure."

"We've got kind of a system going," Patrice added. "It's hard to delegate, now."

Jersey rummaged in the refrigerator for a diet soda. She had to push through piles of food to find one. A 22-pound turkey defrosted on a dishtowel on the bottom shelf; a myriad of salads and desserts, cans of olives and jars of pickles, filled the rest of the shelves. She peeked into the freezer as she straightened up.

"There it is. Thanksgiving wouldn't be the same without your frozen fruit salad, Patrice."

"It's my claim to fame." Her sister laughed.

"Aunt Liz and Uncle Jack will be here tomorrow at ten," Mom said. "Brad and Nikki, and their kids, should be here by eleven. And, we'll eat about three, as usual."

"All right!" Jersey exclaimed. "It'll be great to see everybody again."

Patrice nodded. "Remember when Brad taught us how to ride his two-wheeler?"

"And, the summer we all ran off to the beach everyday, instead of going to summer school!"

"We used to get into so much trouble, the three of us."

"He was more like a big brother, than a cousin."

"It's amazing y'all grew up to be such fine adults," Mom said in mock wonder.

"Y'all," the sisters mimicked. Jersey drawled, "Will you never lose that Tennessee accent, Mama?"

"Will you girls never learn to respect your mother?"

They looked at each other, considering the possibility. "No!" They said together, and broke up, again.

Later, after the turkey was stuffed and the relish platter prepped, Jersey and Patrice shared the sofa, a bowl of popcorn and a newsmagazine show. During commercials, they caught up on each other's lives, Patrice gossiping about old friends. Just as the anchor hosts were bantering their goodnights, Mom came in wearing a familiar terry robe, her hair damp from the shower.

"You girls are sharing your old room," she said. "Towels and extra blankets are in the hall closet. Stay up as late as you like, and don't worry about getting up at any certain time. Goodnight, girls."

"Goodnight, Mom," they said together, avoiding each other's eyes to keep from giggling.

"We've go to stop talking in unison," Jersey whispered.

Patrice snickered. "She tells us the same thing every year."

"As if we might forget where everything is. She hasn't moved a thing since high school."

They laughed, unable to hold back any longer. The blond anchorwoman said goodnight, and Jersey stood, stretching.

"I'm going to get my things from the service porch. I'll lock up back there and meet you upstairs."

She set the popcorn bowl in the sink as she passed through the kitchen. Neither Mom nor Patrice had mentioned Halloween night, she thought with relief. They obviously didn't now what had happened. She was surprised Patrice hadn't been told, but she wasn't going to tell them either.

The two women dressed for bed as they had every night before Jersey sent to college. Patrice slipped into a lacy cotton nightgown, while Jersey pulled on a long-sleeved tee and sweatpants. In high school, they had endured Mom's annual redecorating sprees, their room having been every possible combination of their favorite colors, green and yellow. Finally, Mom had settled on green pinstriped wallpaper and terminally cheery yellow rosebuds on the curtains and spreads. As teens, they had thought the scheme too hokey for words. Jersey folded back the comforter on her bed. It really was lovely, she thought. She'd be sure to thank her mother before she went home Sunday.

Patrice went to turn out the light, and Jersey noticed a fresh bruise above her sister's shoulder blade. Her gown strap barely covered the blue-black spot commingling with a yellow-green one. She had seen many bruises on her sister over the last twenty years, since Patrice and Wade married. That hadn't changed either. Patrice had gotten defensive the few times Jersey mentioned the bruises, so she said nothing now. As they settled under their childhood comforters, Jersey heard her sister turn toward her.

"Did he get in touch with you, Jersey?"

Her throat tightened; maybe Patrice knew, after all. "Who?" She whispered.

"You know who. I hope you aren't too mad about me giving

him your number."

"I wish you had warned me, first."

"He begged me, Jersey. Besides, you would've said no. You would've done the same thing in my place."

"I just would have been better prepared, had I known."

"Then, he did find you." Her sister sounded almost disappointed. "How'd it go?"

"We...settled things. Permanently." Jersey stared into the dark. Finally she asked, "Patrice, what do you remember about Dad, before he left?"

"Not much." She sighed. "After all, we were pretty little when they divorced."

"Do you remember any physical abuse, or anything like that?"

"Hitting each other? No. I do remember they argued a lot, mostly about you. Why, what do you remember?"

"I don't remember much, either. I guess we were too little, like you said."

"What'd you mean, permanently?" Patrice asked.

"I'll tell you and Mom before I leave," Jersey said, rolling away from her sister. She couldn't talk about it, couldn't think about it now.

Sometime during the night, Jenna's voice penetrated her sleep. "Jersey, I'm cold. I don't like it here."

"It's all right, Honey Bunny," she whispered, molding the child's tiny body to her own. "I'm here."

Thanksgiving Day, November 24

Jersey woke to the sound of the shower. Patrice's bed was already made and the room was empty. Jersey remade her own bed, then laid out her clothes while she waited for her turn in the bathroom. She chuckled to herself as she worked. She felt just like she was in high school again, she thought. After showering and doing her hair and makeup, Jersey dressed in a black catsuit, buttoned a floral jumper over it and tied her feet into black walking boots. Then she skipped downstairs to breakfast, the smell of Mom's fresh baked banana muffins wafting through the house and making her stomach rumble. She pushed through the kitchen door, where Mom was sliding the turkey into the oven.

"Morning, Mom." She said, pecking her mother's cheek. "Where's Patrice?"

"Morning, honey. Your sister's polishing the silverware in the dining room. You can set the table, after you've eaten. Mind those rolls on the drain board when you pour your coffee."

Mom took a rag and a bottle of furniture polish from under the sink and left the room. Jersey got a mug from the dishwasher, dropped a coffee bag into it and poured hot water from the kettle. She leaned against the counter, waiting for her coffee to brew, and breathed in the smell of poultry spices and rising yeast rolls. Every available counter space was filled with crystal glassware and Mom's Spode china that she would be setting the table with shortly. Jersey threw her bag into the trash and reached for a muffin, still in the warm tin on the stove. Patrice carried in the silver serving utensils and distributed them into dishes waiting on the island.

"Say, Jersey," she said. "When did you start talking in your sleep?"

"I didn't know I did. What did I say?"

Mom came back in and stowed away the cleaning gear.

"Most of it was whispered," Patrice said. "But, you said something about a bunny."

"You were probably dreaming." Mom patted Jersey's cheek. "You aren't working too hard, are you?"

Jersey shook her head. The front doorbell rang. "I'll get it!" She said, making her escape. She pushed her cup between a couple of bowls as she went.

* * * * *

Alison opened the front door. "Uncle Spencer!" She exclaimed. "You're late. I been waiting and waiting for you."

"Well, here I am." Spencer stepped across the threshold and swung his niece into his arms. Being his day off, he had indulged in comfort, wearing jeans and a green polo shirt. He could smell the citrus-sweet fragrance of roasting fowl. "Mm, doesn't your Mom's turkey smell great? Where is she, anyway?"

"In the den with Scotty. We're watching the parade. Santa Claus isn't here yet, but Bart Simpson was riding a skateboard."

"He was!" He tweaked Alison's nose and set her on the floor. He wondered if Jenna was also watching the parade. Alison stepped up onto his feet and together they walked into the den.

The room was done in cranberry red and navy blue. Scott's citations were on the walls, alongside photos and trophies he and his son had won bike racing. Belinda, in black sweats, lay propped on some large pillows in front of a big-screen television. Scott, Jr. reclined in a Lazy Boy, sporting purple-and-gold gym clothes, and munching tortilla chips and salsa.

"You know if you people didn't watch this stuff, we could

force the networks to show quality programming."

"Hi, Uncle Spencer," Scotty said, around a mouthful of tortilla mush. "You're just in time. The game starts in forty-five minutes."

"Hi ya, kiddo. That was some Homecoming game, you guys-Oof!" He caught a pillow to the gut. "Belinda!"

"How ya doin', Copper?" She jumped up and gave him a playful shot to the ribs. Spencer grabbed her around the shoulders and yanked her ponytail.

"This isn't one of those pin-on jobbies, is it?"

All day, Spencer watched his niece playing and eating and imagined Jenna doing the same things. Belinda had dressed Alison in a red and white jumpsuit with a wide, lace-trimmed collar, red tights and black patent leather shoes. Her long silky curls were kept out of her face by a red bow. Alison ran, danced, laughed, and shouted, imprinting herself on every moment of the day. By the end of dinner, she also wore gravy and cranberry sauce, her tights had a hole in one ankle, and pale tendrils escaped her bow.

Spencer sat on the sofa now, watching her wheel a doll stroller around the front room, careening faster and faster, jeopardizing her baby's safety. He pictured a little girl with copper curls and green eyes playing similar games at her Grandma's and hoped Jenna was enjoying her Thanksgiving. Alison sure enjoyed hers. His mind went round and round - no birth records, no school records, he thought. Something was wrong with the whole picture, but he couldn't quite finger the error. Like finding nine of the ten things wrong in a cartoon puzzle, and not seeing the last item.

Belinda plopped down beside him and handed him a beer.

"You sold any poems, lately, Sis?"

"Cosmopolitan magazine is going to publish one, next month." She watched him watching Alison, until he met her eyes. "You still think about it, too, don't you?"

"Do you ever not think about it?"

"Sometimes, yeah. Her therapist says Ali's dealing with it really well. She doesn't wet her bed anymore, and her nightmares are few and far between. She adjusts, then I adjust."

"I saw Dr. Kaneally, last week. She seems to know what she's doing."

"She told me you stopped by. She's been Ali's lifesaver. Mine, too. Especially now." Belinda shuddered.

"I can't believe that bastard's out on the streets, after only eighteen months."

"Neither can I." Belinda sipped her beer. "I always thought we should have hung him on a piling by his short hairs, left him for gull food."

Spencer laughed, humorlessly. He leaned his head against the wall, swallowing half his beer. He shook his head, sighing. "God, Belinda! I am so sick of it all. I'm fed up with selfish, unfeeling adults using their children."

"You're not one of them, Spence. You're just doing your job."

"I need another slice of pecan pie to swallow this rancor," he said, getting up.

* * * * *

Ward patted his stomach. "Mom, that was the best Thanksgiving dinner yet."

"You say that every year," Patrice said, smiling. She patted her husband's hand.

Jersey watched them, seeing Patti's bruises in her mind's eye. Her nephews had inherited their dad's thick curly hair and slight overbite. Mom and Aunt Liz looked like twins, though there was three years between them. Brad and his wife were both sandy-haired and blue eyed, and had passed their genes on to their brood.

"What's for dessert?" Ben asked.

"That's a growing boy for you." Aunt Liz laughed. "Brad used to be just like him."

Brad rolled his eyes, but laughed. "Who's up for another football game?" He asked.

"The TV kind, or the real thing?" Gabe asked.

"TV, of course."

Ben rose. "I'm in."

The males trooped into the living room. Brad's wife, Nikki, got up and began stacking plates. Jersey passed her those around her. Uncle Jack came in from the kitchen, a toothpick stuck in his mouth. He held the door for Nikki.

"Where are my grandkids?" He bellowed, good-naturedly.

"Oh, Jack," Aunt Liz scolded. "Leave 'em alone. They're playing Monopoly in the girl's old room. Why don't you go watch football with the rest of the guys?"

"While you cats sharpen your claws on the back fence." He shot back, smiling. He followed the sound of grunts and cheers into the living room.

Jersey carried out bowls of leftovers. She held the kitchen door with her heel for Nikki, her hands full of glasses.

"Are you still making those silk floral arrangements, Nikki?"

"I sure am. I cleared nearly twelve hundred dollars, last month. Of course, I had to sit through nearly a dozen craft shows to do it. Thank goodness, the holidays are here. I should quadruple my sales before January one."

"Would you be interested in donating something to a San Diego Jaycee's auction? They sponsor Christmas shopping sprees for underprivileged children, and I'm helping coordinate their annual craft show to raise funds."

"I'm sure I could come up with something. Come by the house Saturday, and I'll see what I've got." A wail came from the dining room. "That's one of mine."

Nikki and Jersey hurried out to find four-year-old Serena crying and holding her fingers. Her seven-year-old brother curled around the doorjamb, looking guilt-stricken.

"Damion stepped on me," Serena wailed.

"I didn't mean to, Mom. I said I'm sorry."

The boy appeared on the verge of tears, himself. Nikki shepherded her little ones out. Jersey sat down at the table with the others where Patrice and Aunt Liz discussed the rising cost of raising teenage boys. Mom sipped her iced tea, her eyes following Nikki and the children.

"I love having little ones around, again," Mom said. "I love listening to them squabble. Both my grandsons are young men, already."

"Ben, Gabe," Patrice called. "Get in here and squabble for your grandma, will you?"

"Thank you, sweetheart."

"Anything to make you happy, Mom."

"Jersey Rae Masters." Aunt Liz fixed her with a mock glare. "When are you going to settle down and give your mother a grand-child?"

She shrugged, smiling stiffly.

"She just hasn't found the right man yet, Liz," Mom said. "When she does, Jersey will settle down."

She smiled, again. Here it comes, she thought. Any minute now, the conversation would turn to their childhood, hers and Patrice's. How lucky she was to have had such a wonderful rela-tionship with her father, someone would say. Patrice left for the living room and Jersey tasted guilt. Patrice had heard the story for years, too. In all the years it was repeated, Jersey had never felt lucky. Today, she felt dirty, and she debated telling everyone what she had done. She saw his face in her mind, saw the horror as he realized she had shot him, the look of utter surprise just before he fell. She pushed away the memory and smiled.

"When, your father was here, Jersey," Aunt Liz began. "You were such a lucky little girl...."

That night, Jersey held Jenna, unable to fall asleep. The little girl's soft body and steady breathing reminded her of what she knew was most important. Jenna depended on her to be strong, to take care of bad dreams and overzealous police officers. Suddenly, she started awake, the sound of heavy footsteps on the stairs. Not again, she thought, pulling Jenna closer. She hoped she wouldn't wake the child with the knocking of her own heart. Footsteps scuffed

along the hall, heading directly for the bedroom. Terror impris-
oned her breath in her lungs. Jenna woke with a yelp.

"Is he comin', Jersey?"

Someone grabbed her shoulder. Jenna shrieked, again.

"Jersey!"

She bolted up. Patrice stood over her, one hand gripping her
shoulder.

"Wake up, for Christ's sake. You're having a nightmare."

"You're telling me." Jersey huddled into her blankets. Patrice
shook her again. "It's okay, I'm awake. I'm okay."

"Do you want to talk about it?"

She pushed her hair out of her face, her emotions on the tips
of her lashes. It would be so easy, she thought, to spill out everything: Halloween, the shooting, and the nightmares. She wanted
to tell.

"No, honestly, Patti. I'm fine. I had a nightmare, but it's fading now. Go back to sleep."

"Good god," she said, climbing back into bed. "It's bad enough
I have to spend the day listening to my favorite Jersey the Wonderful stories. Now, I'm spending my night rescuing you from bad
dreams."

"I'm sorry. Goodnight, Patrice."

Jersey propped herself against her headboard, the little girl
clinging to her. Jenna's eyes fluttered and closed, but she knew she
wouldn't sleep any more, tonight. Pattie's deep breathing soon
filled the silent room. Jersey patrolled the darkness, shadows of a
tree on the wall causing her heart to race. Tomorrow, she vowed.
She would talk to Jenna tomorrow.

Friday, November 25

The house was quiet when Jersey woke. Mom had an early shift at the hospital. Patrice would soon be up to her Macy's nametag in pre-holiday bargain shoppers. Jersey sighed, grateful for the solitude. She didn't want to answer any questions about nightmares or sleeping habits. She went downstairs to make some coffee before she showered.

Jenna must be sleeping still, she thought, waiting for the water to boil. Usually, the little girl jumped into bed with her as soon as the sun came through the curtains. Today, Jersey hoped they would find out what the nightmares were all about.

After breakfast, Jersey threw a blanket coat over blue jeans and a big sweater, and drove out to Seacliff State Beach. No one manned the tollbooth, so she parked her car in a deserted lot and headed down to the sand. Seacliff Beach had been her favorite picnic spot growing up. Its great cliffs, tangled with wildflowers and sea grasses, sheltered a crescent of white sand from the rest of the world. It was a quiet place where she knew she could talk to Jenna without drawing attention. Gulls caroled overhead. A flock of small brown sandpipers danced in the waves, digging for sand crabs. Steel-gray waves broke on shore, in great sheets. A couple of diehard surfers in neon wetsuits attempted to shoot them anyway. Jersey walked halfway to the water and sat down, watching the surfers.

"Jenna, are you with me?" She whispered.

This was so unusual, she thought. She had never had to seek out the little girl. Jenna was always with her. Cold seeped through her jeans and she stood, brushing sticky sand from her seat and legs. She shivered and wrapped her coat around her. Jersey walked along the shore, listening to the sand crunch under her boots. Waves foamed at her feet; the sun was a silver lozenge in the gray sky. Before long, Jenna's hand crept into hers. Her voice was timid, far away.

"Jersey?"

"Good morning, Honey Bunny. I was wondering where you'd gotten to."

"Those bad dreams keep comin' back, now."

"I know, Jenna. I've tried to stop them. I'm sorry, I can't this time."

"You been always takin' care of me, Jersey."

"That's because you're so easy to take care of," she said, smiling. "Most of the time."

A large wave crashed at their feet. Jenna shrieked in terror and bolted across the sand. Jersey chased her, caught her easily. Jenna trembled against her. Jersey held her, murmuring reassurances. She rocked Jenna until her breathing slowed and she loosened her grip.

"That big wave really scared you, didn't it, Honey Bunny?"

"Uh huh." Her thumb stole toward her mouth. Jersey held her hands, gently but firmly, in her lap.

"Why did it scare you?" She asked. "Can you tell me?"

Jenna shook her head. "I don't want to."

"Okay. You don't have to." Her heart leapt in relief. She didn't want to know.

Then, the child opened up and word pictures flooded Jersey's heart and mind. She saw Jenna and her daddy playing at this same beach on a hot summer afternoon. Jenna was a few years younger. They built sandcastles and splashed in the surf. All at once, a large wave charged Jenna, dragging her off her feet. She struggled as the wave flipped her topsy-turvy. Salt water stung her mouth and nose; it burned her eyes and lungs. Jenna floundered, desperate for air, then just as suddenly the wave slammed her onto the sand at

Daddy's feet. He stood at the water's edge, Jersey saw, close enough to pull the child out. Instead, he stood laughing at her.

"He didn't help me," Jenna whimpered. "I was so scared."

Jersey hugged her tight. "He can't hurt you any more, Honey Bunny."

She rose and took the child's hand, and they walked up onto the concrete pier. She bought them a hot chocolate at the only snack stand open this time of year. Candy bars and Cokes shared the fridge with smelt and anchovies. Fishermen, bundled in coats and caps, hung their poles over the peeling wooden rails. Jersey couldn't tell if they were having good luck or bad.

She led Jenna to a weather-beaten bench, facing the sea. A gulf of sadness swirled between them that Jersey was reluctant to cross. She had come for Jenna's memories, now she wasn't sure she wanted them. Jenna's terror could too easily become her own. She knew Jenna's father had hurt her, but Jersey couldn't bear to see what she feared was horrible abuse. Her hands shook, so did her insides. She took several deep salty breaths, trying to steady her nerves. Behind her, Jenna slurped hot chocolate.

"What's the matter, Jersey?"

She considered the question, then plunged ahead. "I want to ask you something, but I'm afraid. I want you to tell me what you remember about your daddy."

"No, I don't want to, Jersey." Jenna shook her head, her chin quivering. "I don't like to."

"I know. I don't like this, either. But, I think your memories are causing the bad dreams. I can stop the dreams, if I know why we're having them. I hope."

Jenna stared out at the ocean, chewing her thumbnail. Jersey watched a gull rummage in a nearby garbage can. Pickings were slim, though, and it moved on.

"Do you have those memories, Jenna?"

"I don't know," she whispered. "I don't think so."

Jersey waited. She couldn't think of an easier way. "Did you ever tell anyone he hurt you?"

"Uh huh."

"You did? Who did you tell?"

"Maybe, that mommy?"

"What did you tell her?"

Jenna took her back to the big sunny kitchen. Jersey knew it well, she had grown up here. The wooden table and chairs painted glossy yellow, stood in the center of the room and creamy yellow curtains billowed at the windows. Jersey saw her mother standing before the sink, washing dishes. She wore cotton peddle-pushers and a polka dot shell in tangerine; her auburn hair swirled around her shoulders. Jenna sat on the table. Suddenly, Jersey was sitting with her, watching Jenna's little feet in black patent leather shoes swing back and forth above the yellow-flecked linoleum.

"Daddy tickled me on the grass in the backyard," Jenna said. "And, he covered me up and pushed on me bottom too hard and that's why my bottom hurts right now."

"I hope he didn't get your good dress dirty," Mom said. "Roughhousing like that." She rinsed a bowl and stacked it in the dish drainer. "Run see what your sister's doing, okay?"

"I don't think she understood you," Jersey whispered.

The ocean air felt colder, the surf crashed below them. Jersey looked down at Jenna, her heart lodged behind her ribs like a stone.

"Daddy got mad at me for telling that mommy. He pushed my face in the water in the bathtub, and he didn't let me get up until Patrice comed in and saw me."

"He tried to drown you!" Jersey left the bench to lean over the railing, nausea overwhelming her. She had always known Daniel Miller was a disgusting human being. She was glad she had killed him.

"Are you mad at me, too, Jersey?"

She wrapped the child in her arms. "Of course not, Honey Bunny. I could never be mad at you. I'm mad at myself. I shouldn't have pushed you to remember." She smiled, then. "Let's forget all of this and get a pizza."

"Okay." Jenna smiled too, but reluctantly.

"Come on. Pizza with stuffed crust?" Jersey swung their hands back and forth. "It's just you me, Honey Bunny, doing our jobs like always. I take care of you; you take care of having fun." Jenna began to sparkle. "That's my girl," Jersey said.

Mom's dusty Volvo was in the driveway when Jersey pulled in. It was late and the house was dark. After pizza, Jersey had taken Jenna to a Disney double feature where they laughed and forgot about ugly memories. Now, Jenna slept peacefully. Mom must be sleeping too, Jersey thought, closing the back door quietly. She wrote a note on the pizza box for Mom to help herself, then she went up to bed. She had the room to herself tonight, Patrice having rejoined her family.

* * * * *

"You can't get me! You can't get me!"

Giggling and singing, three-year-old Jenna Marie skipped across her backyard. Roses and pine trees bordered the green lawn, scenting the clear summer air. Jenna wore a pink-striped sundress and pink bloomers; her shoes and socks were under the kitchen table. Jenna glanced back at the house. Was he comin', yet?

She ran for the far corner of the yard, hiding behind a stack of firewood twice as high as she was. She heard the screen door bang shut and her tummy fluttered with excitement. Jenna peeked out to see if Daddy was looking for her.

"Where's my Baby Girl?" Daddy called, affectionately. She ducked, giggling uncontrollable. "Now where do you suppose that little giggle box got to? Is she hiding in the garage?"

Jenna clapped her hands over her mouth, pins of anticipation pricking her arms and neck. She heard his shoes crunching on the gravel drive. She tiptoed out, looking for him.

"Gotcha!"

Daddy pounced on her from behind, catching her under her arms and swinging her high into the air. Jenna shrieked with laughter, throwing her legs out as the world dropped away. She tipped her head back and looked up at him, grinning. Daddy swung her hips over his head and balanced her atop his head, his long dark hair tickling her bare tummy. He held her wrists in his huge hands. Jenna gazed around her; she was queen of the world. Daddy gave her an upside-down kiss, then whirled her like a top. Jenna held on, laughing madly. When Daddy rolled her to the ground she was dizzy, but she tried to run anyway. Crash! She lost her balance and sprawled on the grass, giggling and watching the world spin around her. Daddy dropped down beside her, laughing heartily. He stretched out on his side, bracing his head on one hand, and resting the other on her stomach. He leaned over and kissed her temple.

"Mm, your hair smells so good," he said, nuzzling her cheek. "I love you, Baby Girl. You're the only one who understands me."

"I love you too, Daddy." Jenna touched his cheek, her chubby fingers pale against his tan skin.

"I know you do." Tears crept into his voice, and worry swelled in her heart. Jenna kissed him.

"Don't be sad, Daddy," she pleaded.

"I'm not sad when I'm with you, Baby Girl. I'm always so happy when we're together."

Jenna smiled. Daddy kissed her mouth and cradled her head in the crook of his arm, gazing into her eyes. Happiness flushed through her, like a warm blast of air. Jenna was afraid her insides might break open from this happy feeling rushing through her. She felt so special, and so safe, when Daddy looked at her like this.

"You are my special girl," Daddy said. He slipped his hand inside her shirt, stroking her lightly. He kissed her again, urgently. "Oh, Jenna," he groaned.

She could scarcely breathe, her heart was pounding too hard. Her skin tingled where his fingers brushed her stomach. She pressed closer to him, wanting him to keep loving her. Daddy groaned again and slid his hand into her bloomers. He touched her through her panties. A sharp hot tickle shot through her. Jenna fell back, uncertain, searching his face.

"Daddy?"

"It's okay, Baby Girl," he said, kissing her again. "I just want to love you."

"I just want you to love me too, Daddy." Jenna was breathless. His fingers on her bottom made her weak and hot all over.

"I love you, Baby Girl. I love you so much."

He pulled his tee shirt over his head and spread it on the grass. He laid her down on it and slid off her bloomers and panties. Jenna lay on the warm shirt that smelled like Daddy, unsure what to do. He'd never loved her like this before, and he looked so strange. His cheeks were too red and he trembled all over, breathing hard. She watched him fumble with his belt, the buckle jingling. He slid down his zipper, and then Daddy rolled on top of her. Jenna couldn't breathe under his weight. She was scared, now. She looked for the house, but they were behind the woodpile where Mommy couldn't see them. Daddy grunted, pushing something hot and hard into her bottom. But, it was too big and it tore at her, hurting a lot. What was he trying to put in her, she wondered?

"Ow, Daddy!" Jenna tried to scramble away, but he was too heavy. His breath thundered around her. He kept pushing, harder and harder. "Ow! Don't Daddy; it's hurting me. Don't!"

But, Daddy couldn't hear her; he was breathing too loud. He shoved into her, again and again, crying out sharply. Then, he slid down next to her, gasping. His face on hers was slick with sweat. Jenna lay very still beneath him; she couldn't move because his arm pinned her down. Her bottom hurt worse than anything she could remember. What had she done to make him hurt her like this, she wondered? It must have been something really bad.

At last Daddy lifted his head and looked into her eyes. He didn't look mad, at all. Jenna knew his look of love. Maybe it was all right now, she thought. He hoisted himself up on one elbow and brushed her damp golden curls of her cheeks. He kissed her cheeks and her eyelids, her forehead and her mouth.

"I love you so much, Baby Girl," he whispered.

Jenna wanted to cry. She hurt worse when she moved, so she lay as still as she could. Why had he done that? Daddy raised himself to his knees and fastened his pants. Then, he helped her to her feet. Jenna stood very still, aching. Sticky stuff ran down her legs and Daddy wiped it away with his tee shirt. The white cloth came away streaked with blood. Jenna saw it and shrieked in alarm. Daddy followed her gaze to the stains. His face filled with horror. He looked back at her, tears welling in his eyes.

"My.... Baby Girl," he whimpered. "What did I do to you? What did I do?"

He wadded his shirt in his hands, staring at it in disbelief. Tears slid down his cheeks. He dropped the shirt in the grass and reached for her, but Jenna shrank back. Was he going to do it again? Daddy sat back on his heels, holding out his hand.

"Jenna. Baby Girl. I'm so sorry." His voice broke into sobs. "I'm so sorry, Baby Girl, please forgive me. I didn't mean to hurt you. I'm so sorry. Please forgive me."

Jenna didn't hesitate. She came to him wrapped her arms around his neck, tears starting in her own eyes. " 's okay, Daddy. Don't cry. It doesn't hurt me so bad," she assured him, patting his shoulders with her little hands. "See? I'm better now. Don't cry, 'kay, Daddy?"

He wiped his eyes on his tee shirt, then helped her into her clothes. He held her hand as they walked back to the house.

* * * * *

Jersey shoved back her blankets and tried to stand, but her knees buckled under her. She scrambled into the bathroom on hands and knees and threw up in the commode. She crumpled on the bathmat, resting her hot cheek on the cool linoleum. Jenna curled into a corner, the picture of betrayal and abandonment.

Jersey crawled to her, taking the child in her arms. Jenna clung to her, crying.

"So that's what he did to you," Jersey whispered. The bastard had violated his little girl, then he cried and she comforted him. Disgust roiled in her stomach, and she hung her head over the bowl, again.

"I didn't want him to, Jersey. I didn't, honest."

"I know, Honey Bunny." Emptiness ached inside her. She had no words to comfort the little girl, so she just held her. Soft knocking penetrated Jersey's thoughts.

"Jersey, is everything all right?" Mom called.

Humiliation smacked her, how could she tell her mother about this? "Yes, Mom. I'm fine."

"Are you sick?"

"I guess I overdid the holiday, that's all."

"Okay, then. I'm needed at the hospital. My regular shift starts at eight, so I won't be home until late this afternoon. Have a good day, dear. Bye."

She listened to her mother's footsteps fading away. She heard the back door close, then the car door. Jersey sat on the bathroom floor, the sour-sweet odor of vomit in her nostrils, and held Jenna. What should she do now, she wondered?

Saturday, November 26

Jersey pulled into her own driveway and switched off the motor and lights. Midnight folded around her, familiar as a favorite blanket. She leaned back in her seat, still feeling the engine vibrate through her arms. God it was great to be home, she thought, and let her head loll against the seatback. The last twenty-four hours swam around her. She couldn't stop thinking about Daniel Miller raping his three-year-old daughter; every time she thought of it, she felt sick again. It had been so hard to act normally around Mom. Finally, she had just left. Jenna had curled into a corner of her subconscious, mute and unmoving. Her silence frightened Jersey, and she regretted opening old wounds. She felt helpless, useless to alleviate the little girl's pain. At the same time, she felt relieved. Ignoring Jenna's pathetic posture gave her some respite from the tortuous memories.

Someone tapped at her window. Jersey started and looked out. Spencer Phillips peered back at her, looking like he had slept in his suit. She rolled down her window, wondering how she had gotten into this Columbo movie.

"Detective Phillips," she snapped. "How thoughtful of you to welcome me home."

"My pleasure, Miss Masters." He returned in kind.

Jersey flung open her door, catching him under the chin with the window frame. "Oh, excuse, me," she said.

She went to unlock the trunk. Spencer rubbed his chin; the skin was broken, but he wasn't bleeding. He bent to look in her car; the interior, lit with dome light, smelled of vanilla. And, was empty. Jersey set her bags on the driveway and slammed the trunk.

"Where's your daughter, Miss Masters? Still with your family?"

"Where are your manners, detective?" She hoisted her bags and headed for her front door. "I've had a very long drive, and an even longer weekend. I'd like to go to bed."

Spencer grabbed her elbow, spilling her luggage. "Where is your daughter?" He demanded.

"I don't have to tell you that." She spat, jerking her arm away.

"You and Jenna are supposed to appear in court tomorrow morning. One phone call to Judge Morgan and I'll have your bail revoked. I won't hesitate to wake her."

"Don't threaten me." Jersey's green eyes narrowed, dangerously. "Wake the judge, if you're going to. When you have your arrest warrant, ring my bell. Otherwise, goodnight."

She retrieved her suitcases from the walk and marched into her house. Spencer stood glaring after her. He had been waiting here since early afternoon; his heart had flipped and swelled with the anticipation of seeing and speaking to Jenna for the first time. Judge Morgan had insisted the two appear before her; it had never occurred to him that Jersey wouldn't comply. He rubbed his chin again, the scratch stung at his touch. He turned on his heel and trudged to his car, slinging himself into the driver's seat and reaching for his cell phone. Jersey Masters had asked for this fight. He was happy to oblige her, dammit.

Ouch! Something sharp dug into his backside. Spencer hoisted himself up, swiped the seat and extracted his headphones dangling from his personal stereo. They were bent and twisted now, he wouldn't be using them again. How would Jenna feel about her mother going back to jail, he thought now. Did he want to be responsible for putting Jersey there? He dragged his thumb across his forehead, thinking. He threw the ruined earphones at the dashboard, then slammed the steering wheel. Ugh! The woman was maddening!

What if Mateo was right and Jersey couldn't bring the girl home? What if Jenna was dead now, and he could have prevented it by following Jersey to Santa Cruz? Had he sacrificed the child for a turkey dinner and pecan pie? He slugged his knee; leaned back, breathing in and out, measuring his heartbeats. Don't trip over any conclusions, he told himself. Find your rationality. He started the engine, then booted the computer. If he was required to play Mohammed, he must locate the mountain. He knew from court files that Jersey's mother was Marguerite Wilson, he thought, accessing DMV records. Bingo! South Sycamore Drive, Santa Cruz. He shifted into reverse.

The northbound freeways were dark and empty for the most part. Spencer drove all night, focused only on the blue reflector dots rushing at him. He stopped twice for coffee eye-openers and once, inside county limits, for directions. Then, he backtracked to a suburb called Live Oak. At 6:10 a.m., Phillips cruised down S. Sycamore Street, behind a faded orange Volvo, checking house numbers. A winter sun bleached a gray sky. The neighborhood was World War II-era bungalows built side by side on postage stamp lawns. He expected to see mothers in aprons and pin curls, leaving their wash lines for the back fence and the gossip of the day. He imagined the wholesome lifestyles led behind those gleaming picture windows, curtained for privacy. Then, he shivered with a sudden chill, thinking of Jenna growing up in a neighborhood such as this, realizing the horror that such picturesque neighborhoods could secret.

At the end of the street, the Volvo pulled into the driveway of a rambling two-story house, its address the same as he had been looking for. Spencer parked at the opposite curb and watched a woman in hospital whites get out of the Volvo and walk across the front lawn to pick up a newspaper. He recognized her from the snapshot on Jersey's dresser: Marguerite Wilson, her white-streaked bangs vouching her identity. She started back to her car, then rounded the corner of the house, heading for the back.

Spencer exited his car, his back and thighs groaning from the long hours behind the wheel, and tried to brush out permanent creases in his trousers. He jogged across the street and up the gravel drive, glancing into the Volvo as he passed it. No one was in it, though Jenna could have been left with a sitter, he thought. He hurried after her grandma. Mrs. Wilson was just unlocking her back door when he came into sight. He cleared his throat, proffering his badge as he approached.

"Good morning, ma'am. I'm Detective Spencer Phillips; San Diego Police. You are Jersey Masters' mother?"

"San Diego!" She exclaimed, distress creasing her face. "Has something happened to my daughter? Is Jersey all right?"

"Yes. Whoa, Mrs. Wilson. I apologize. Jersey is fine. I'm not here about her."

"Well, thank goodness." She sank into a nearby lawn chair. "Jersey lives so far away, I worry something will happen and I won't be able to get to her right away." She squinted up at him. "If you're not here about Jersey, what do you want?"

Spencer positioned himself between her and the morning sun. He took in the yard at a glance; a pine grove buttressing a huge expanse of yellowing winter grass. Old roses lined the property fences. An ocean tang hung in the air.

"In a manner of speaking, I am here about Jersey," he said. "I'm working the Daniel Miller case. He was shot and killed Halloween night."

"Daniel is dead?" She wet her lips that were suddenly white, and lowered her eyes. "Does Jersey know?"

"Yes, ma'am. She shot him."

"Jersey shot him! When? How?" She searched his face, wanting to understand. "I can't believe it! How did it happen?"

"Jersey claims he showed up out of the blue, and refused to leave. She claims it was self-defense."

"Why, Jersey was just here for the whole weekend. As a matter of fact, she only went home last night, and she never said one word. Imagine him showing up, after all these years. And, right in her home, you said. She never said one word...." Her voice trailed away.

"Mrs. Wilson?" She appeared to withdraw into herself "Mrs. Wilson!" Her attention returned to him. "I want to help your daughter. I don't believe she intended to kill Miller. But, I need Jenna to tell me what happened that night."

"No one's called her that in a very long time, detective. I'm surprised she told you. Though, I suppose it's a matter of public record."

"She called 911 after the shooting. I believe she witnessed what happened, and is a key to deciding this case."

"A witness? I thought you said she shot him."

"Jersey shot him, ma'am. I'm trying to get Jenna's statement, but your daughter keeps blocking me. Will you allow me to talk to her?"

"I told you, she went home yesterday. To San Diego."

Spencer felt as if he'd missed the punch line of the joke. Mrs. Wilson was looking confused, as well. What was he missing?

"Jersey is at home, yes," he said. "I spoke to her last night. But, Jenna wasn't with her. That's why I came here today."

"Jenna wasn't with her." Mrs Wilson repeated his words under her breath. She looked up at him. "You're speaking of Jersey and Jenna as if they were two people."

"Jersey doesn't have a daughter named Jenna?" He groaned, inwardly.

"Mr. Phillips, Jersey is Jenna."

Air rushed from his lungs; he gasped to refill them. "I beg your pardon!"

"My daughter was born Jenna Marie Miller. She changed her name to Jersey Rae Masters in college. I can tell you, it took us some time to get used to the change, but we adapted. She's been Jersey so long now, I hardly remember she ever went by Jenna."

Spencer cupped his face in his hands, snapping them away. Rivera had called this one, he thought. Jersey Masters was a head case, after all.

"Daniel Miller was not her lover, was he?"

She bristled. "What a disgusting assumption. Daniel was my husband, Jersey's father."

"I'm sorry," he whispered. He backed away, his mind reeling. For three weeks, he had chased a phantom, a figment of Jersey Masters' imagination. No wonder he had found no records for Jenna. No records existed, because there was no little girl; hadn't been for more than twenty years. Rivera had been right; he couldn't believe it.

Mrs. Wilson stood and fished in her pocket for her house key, then closed him out with a bang. Spencer continued to back away, his shoes crunching gravel. Somehow, he made it into his car and onto the highway. He remembered nothing of his trip home, his mind numbed and whirling with the truth. Jersey was Jenna. Ms. Kirby had said to know Jersey was to know Jenna. She said she could tell Jenna had been abused by looking at her. Dr. Kaneally had said dissociation occurred in early childhood; the greater the trauma, the younger the victim, the easier the psyche split. But, he didn't believe in split personalities. Which meant there was no little girl who needed to be rescued. His heart mourned the truth.

At last, he parked his car under his carport and wearily climbed the stairs to his apartment. Though it was the middle of the afternoon, he fell into bed and was instantly asleep.

Sunday, November 27

"Jersey, do you think he's comin', yet?"

Two little girls huddled on a narrow bed. A street lamp shone through faded curtains, illuminating bare white walls and a wooden toy chest that hulked in a corner. Through the open window, crickets sang in the still summer night. On the twin bed next to them, Patrice slept fitfully. The two little girls could see her clearly in the silver light. She had kicked off her covers; her sun-browned arms and legs sprawled over the rumpled sheet. Her brown bangs clung to her damp forehead. The rest of her hair was still caught up in the ponytail Mommy had done this morning.

"I don't think he's comin', yet." Jersey whispered.

"Maybe, he won't be comin', this time?"

"He's always comin', Jenna. You just stay back there, where he can't see you."

"But, I don't like it that he hurts you."

"He doesn't hurt me so much, now. Just stay back there."

The knob rattled and the door swung open. Both girls jumped. Jersey felt Jenna shrink away from her. Better for her, Jersey thought. She closed her eyes, lying still; listening to his foot falls on the bare floor. He would be mad if she was awake. He hurt her more when he was mad. The bed sagged behind her, and her heart lurched. She rolled away, pretending she was asleep, but making room for him. He lay down, drawing her against him. He laid his cheek on hers, his whiskers scratching her. His breath, warm on her face, smelled like spoiled fruit.

"Hey, Baby Girl. Are you asleep? Of course, you are."

She breathed in and out, through her nose. She squeezed her eyes tight shut, clenching her teeth in anticipation. His hand grazed her shoulder; he fumbled with the buttons on her nightshirt.

"Why does your mother insist on dressing you in these damn pajamas?"

He stripped her and tossed away her clothes, her shirt buttons skittering on the floor. He kissed her cheek and ran his hand down her naked chest, over her bare thighs. Jersey breathed tightly, holding very still. Daddy kissed her shoulder and nuzzled her hair.

"Daddy's here," he crooned. "Don't be afraid, Baby Girl."

His stale breath washed her face; choked her. But, she knew better than to cough or move away. His hand caressed her, again. She took a deep breath, held it, let it go.

"You're the most beautiful baby girl in the whole world. I'm so lucky to be your Daddy."

His hand braced her hip. Get ready, get ready, she chanted, silently. He pushed himself hard against her bottom. Jersey breathed through gritted teeth. Tears leaked through her lashes. She prayed he wouldn't find them.

"You want me, too, don't you, Baby Girl?" He whispered. "Tell me you want me, too."

Here was her cue; her voice came ragged, no matter how she tried to control it. "Yes, Daddy," she whispered, as the searing pain jabbed into her core. "I want you to."

* * * * *

"No!" Jenna sprang out of sleep. "Daddy, don't! Jersey! Jersey, help me!"

She scrambled out of bed and dashed through the hall into Jersey's bedroom. She wasn't in her bed. She had folded back her covers, but she wasn't sleeping there.

"Jersey?" She called, but she got no answer. Jenna began to cry. "I'm scared, Jersey. Where are you?"

She crept to the closet door. The bathroom door was closed, no light on under it. She went back into the hall and looked downstairs - no lights on down there, either.

"Jersey?" Her voice trembled; tears warmed her cheeks. "Jer-r-sey!"

Jenna tiptoed down the stairs; her eyes wide and wet, breathing through parted lips. Where's Jersey? Where's Jersey? She stole the rest of the way down and opened the study door.

"Jersey?" Her voice echoed in the dark room. Where'd she go? Jersey never left her by herself. Where'd she go? "Jersey!"

She curled into Jersey's desk chair, pulling Jersey's lap robe around her. It smelled like Jersey and she felt better, a little bit. Jenna sat up and fiddled with the computer mouse. She ran it over the hills of the foam pad, making engine sounds with her lips. She stretched around with her other hand and turned on the computer. The screen bathed her in gray light; the machine whirring as it went through its start-up program. She typed BABYGIRL, then clicked open her file the way Jersey had taught her, last summer, when she got big enough.

JERSEYWHEREAREYOU?IMSCARED.

Jenna pulled off a little card, taped to the side of the computer, looked at it and smiled. She knew what she could do. She reached across the desk for Jersey's telephone.

He answered on the third ring. "Spencer Phillips."

"Are you that p'lceman what came at my house?"

"Who is this?" He snapped.

" 's Jenna. You're that p'lceman what did come at my house?"

Jenna, he thought? Jenna Miller? What game was this? "I'm not amused, Miss Masters. It's the middle of the damn night."

"Jersey's gone. I'm lookin' for her, but she's nowhere."

"What do you mean, Jersey's gone?"

"Jersey, she's not here." Fresh tears choked her and his heart wavered. He knew her voice like he knew his own. "I looked all over. She's gone."

He cupped his face in his free hand, sighing. "Do you want

me to come over?"

"Yeah, I want you to," she cried. "I looked all over. I can't find her."

Spencer hung up and reached for blue jeans and a tee shirt. He donned them quickly, grabbed his keys and ran out of his apartment. His heart raced ahead of him. After all these weeks, he was about to come face to face with Jenna Miller. He slammed his car into gear, and reality hit him. How could it be Jenna, he realized, caught by a red light on Front street. Jenna was a figment, Jersey's concoction. Marguerite Wilson had told him they were one and the same.

So, who would he find at Jersey Master's home? Suspicion snatched him. Maybe, this was a ploy to keep him from calling the judge. Jersey couldn't hide the truth any longer, so she had decided to give him what he wanted. But, how could she? Would she present him with a little girl, introduce her as Jenna? Was she awaiting him with a gun? Why hadn't he thought to bring his own?

Spencer pulled into her driveway, behind Jersey's Mustang. The house was dark and he approached, cautiously. Her front door was unlocked; he pulled back in surprise. Jersey never left her door unlocked. He peered inside, wishing again for his gun. Downstairs was dark and silent. He glanced above to the second floor. Jenna's bedroom door was ajar and soft light spilled into the hall. Keeping his back to the wall, he took the stairs three at a time, his heart hammering in his chest. His hand trembled as he pushed open the bedroom door. He had chased her for weeks. And, there she was!

She sat curled against the headboard, clutching her great black bear. Pink pillows framed her like drifts of cotton candy. She wore a pale pink cotton nightdress, sprinkled with tiny rosebuds. Her little-girl eyes fastened on his and his heart constricted. She made a convincing picture.

"May I come in?"

She nodded. He advanced to the foot of the bed, before she

shrank into her pillows. Her eyes widened and her lips parted in fear. He had seen Alison look at him with those eyes.

"It's all right, Jenna." He said. "I'm not going to hurt you. How about if I sit right on this corner of the bed?"

"No, I don't want you to," she whimpered.

"How about in one of your little chairs, back here. May I sit here?" He slid out the chair and sat down, resting his elbows on his knees. "Is this all right?"

"Uh huh."

Her voice caught him; he had been listening to it for weeks. If she was acting, he thought, she was damn good at it. Her breathing was rapid and shallow and he crooned to her, fearing she might hyperventilate. When she was visibly calmer, breathing evenly, he began his questions.

"Tell me about the night you shot your father." If she was acting, he hoped to trip her up.

"Was Halloween," Jenna said. Her gaze never left his. "I ate the peanut butter cups, but I didn't go trick-or-treating."

"I like peanut butter cups, too," he said, with a smile. "Tell me about Daniel Miller coming here."

"Daddy." Her lip quivered. "He didn't s'posed to come here. Jersey said he didn't s'posed to come here."

"What did he want? Did he tell you?"

She closed her eyes, trapping the horror inside. She shook her, no.

"Your father didn't hurt you, that night, did he?"

"No, not that time." She looked fretful.

"He'd hurt you before, though, hadn't he?"

"I can't tell you." She stared down at her coverlet, mortified.

"That's okay. What happened when you saw your daddy at the door?"

"Jersey, she just dropped our candy. Um, cause she didn't know it was Daddy. But, it was."

"And, you didn't want him here, did you? Did you tell him to leave?"

Jenna nodded, her eyes widening with recall, and she hugged her bear. "Jersey, she got real mad and she called him that bad word."

Spencer smiled into his fist. Jersey using colorful language didn't surprise him. "But, he didn't leave. And, that made you angry, didn't it?"

"I was so scared," she whimpered. "Jersey yelled, 'go away!' But, he just came in our house."

"And, that's when you got the gun?"

"Because he kept comin' in our house." She nodded. "Jersey got that gun and Daddy, he was comin' up here by my bedroom." She shuddered, her eyes closed.

Spencer pressed forward. "And, that's when you shot him, isn't it?"

"I didn't want to." Tears slipped through her lashes. "But, Jersey, she did shoot him with that gun, and Daddy just fell down."

That was Masters' version of what happened, he thought, told in little-girl fashion. He sat back, cupping his face in his hands. He believed her every word, heaven help him. Dissociation was a remarkable survival skill, according to the book Dr. Kaneally had lent him. Jenna Miller was a real little girl, frozen in time by her father's hideous deeds. Spencer exhaled through his hands. She had to say it; he had to be sure.

"Jenna," he whispered. She looked into his eyes. "Tell me the truth. Your daddy didn't hurt you, that night. But, he hurt you before, didn't he?"

"I can't tell you. I can't tell you." She cried, burying her face in her bear.

"It's all right," he said, his heart wringing. "You don't have to tell me. I already know."

She looked up in surprise, and fear. "How you are knowing that?"

"I'm a policeman. It's my job to know when daddies hurt their little girls."

Jenna smiled, her brow relaxing.

"When did you last see Jersey?" He asked.

"When I'm going to sleep, last night. She tucked me in my bed and read me the story and kissed me goodnight. And, then I had that bad dream and I was scared, cause Jersey wasn't here no places where I looked."

"Jersey takes good care of you, doesn't she? Is she your gatekeeper personality?"

"I don't know." She shrugged, obviously puzzled. "She's just my Jersey. She just be's takin' care of me."

"You like Jersey, I can tell."

"Uh huh. She made me this bedroom and she buyed me all my toys, and she takes me to the movies and I get a candy, and we go to the beach and roller skating there and pretty soon, Jersey says we can go at Mexico again, cause I like it there."

She paused and Spencer chuckled, reminded of Alison. Six-year-olds had amazing lung capacity, he thought.

"I know a secret," she whispered.

"What's that, Jenna?"

"Jersey, she says nobody can see me, cause I'm livin' in a grownup." She gave him a shy smile.

"I can see you, Jenna," he assured her. Spencer laughed out loud. "I've waited a long time to meet you."

"You're teasing me." She yawned, openly. "I'm getting more sleepy, now."

"Do you want me to stay with you, until you fall asleep?"

Her face crumpled and she shook her head no. Concern welled in him, and he rose from the little chair, stepping toward her, meaning to comfort her.

"No, NO!" Jenna shrieked, cowering into her pillows.

Damn fool! He backed away, cursing himself. Why had he done that? Hadn't Alison taught him anything about making sudden moves?

"I'm sorry, Jenna. I'm sorry. I won't hurt you, I promise. Look, I'm way back here, now. See? I won't hurt you."

"I don't want you to, I don't want you to." She sobbed. She

couldn't hear him. "Where's Jersey? I want Jersey. Why did she leave me? Why'd she leave?" Her voice trailed into singsong. Jenna rocked herself. "Where's Jersey, where's Jersey, where's Jersey?"

Spencer retreated into the hallway, cursing himself, again. How could he have been so stupid? He could hear her whimpering all the way down the stairs. Jersey's study door was open and he closed it without thinking. Street lamps lit the living room through shuttered windows; the rest of the house was black. A faint odor of fried chicken hung in the air, the aroma turning his stomach. His sneakers squeaked on the smooth entry floor, then were muffled by the living room carpet. He sank into one of Jersey's cream linen sofas, still cursing his thoughtlessness. He had no more doubts that Jenna had told him the truth.

"Damn you, Daniel Miller," he whispered. "I hope you're rotting in hell."

His drooping eyelids snapped open. Where was Jersey, he wondered? Dr. Kaneally's book had said the gatekeeper personality remained in control at all cost. Why had Jersey suddenly left the child alone? Could he really fault her for it, he thought? She wasn't Jenna's mother, after all. She was Jenna. While at the same time, she wasn't.

Monday, November 28

Spencer awoke with a start, daylight flooding Jersey's living room. Just when he had fallen asleep, he couldn't remember. He turned his wrist over, but his watch wasn't there. He sat up and found it lying on the coffee table, 7:30 a.m. His sneakers sat neatly underneath the table, though he didn't remember putting them there, either. His neck felt as if he had slept on a stone pillow instead of Jersey's overstuffed sofa. He turned his head - right, left - his tight muscles complaining. His stomach growled and he realized he had eaten his last meal Sunday afternoon, before his impulsive trip to Santa Cruz.

He rubbed himself awake, wondering how Jenna was doing; he thought of checking on her, then thought better of it. After her reactions last night, she should find him downstairs, on safe ground. His stomach gnawed him, again. He could fix them breakfast while he waited for her, he decided. His stomach seconded the idea. Spencer rose unsteadily, stretching his oxygen-starved limbs, and headed into the kitchen. He recalled seeing a bag of coffee in Jersey's freezer.

Coffee, the wonder brew, he thought. He hummed a commercial jingle as he scooped granules of Colombian blend into a paper filter and poured water into the machine. Minutes later, the redolent scent teased his nostrils and frustrated the beast of hunger. He held a turquoise-glazed mug under the amber stream, then carried his cup with him into the bathroom, sipping generously on his way. He was surprised his kidneys had anything left to give after his thirty-six hour fast. Shuffling through the laundry room from the bathroom, he noted the tidiness; lint-free machines, cleaning products lined up evenly on the shelf above, no stray soap flakes or dust anywhere. Jenna now stood in the middle of the kitchen, still wearing her pink nightgown, and a slightly dazed expression. Her chestnut curls sprang from her head.

"Good morning, little lady," he said, wanting to alert her to his presence without panicking her. "Did you have a nice sleep?"

Her brows collided. "What are you doing here?"

"Jersey?"

"Yes. What are you doing here?"

He cupped his free hand over his mouth and let it drop, disappointment seized him, overwhelmed him. "Jenna called me last night," he said. "She couldn't find you. She was frightened. I didn't feel right leaving her alone."

She dropped her gaze to the right, searching inwardly. "You can go home, now. I'm here. I'll take care of Jenna."

"Why did you leave her alone, last night?"

"I don't know." Raw anguish darkened her eyes and she shook her head, her dark curls brushing her cheeks. "Nothing like this has ever happened."

Spencer moved to the counter, traced his thumb over terra cotta grout. To spite himself, he found he was drawn by her utter loss. "I make good coffee, for a cop. Let me pour you a cup."

She stood mutely, staring into herself. Spencer poured her coffee, then led her to the table and guided her into a chair. He set the mug in front of her and sat beside her, noticing crumbs on the walnut surface.

"What's the last thing you remember?"

"Putting Jenna to bed." She rubbed her forehead with her fingertips. "What day is it?"

"It's Monday, the twenty-eighth. Is that the day it's supposed to be?" Jersey nodded. "Have you blacked out like this before?"

She shook her head no, and sipped her coffee. "This is good," she murmured.

"I drove to Santa Cruz, yesterday. Your mother straightened me out on something."

"I can imagine."

"Why did you tell me Jenna was your daughter?"

"I said she is my child. You assumed she was my daughter."

"You knew I wouldn't understand the difference," he said.

"I knew you wouldn't understand, period. You still don't, even after seeing."

"Explain it to me, then."

Jersey took a long swallow. "I don't think I can."

"I understand sexual abuse. My niece was molested two years ago, by a neighborhood paper boy."

"I'm sorry. No child should have to go through that."

He cupped her hand. "No, they shouldn't."

Jersey pulled away, huddling into her chair. Spencer's heart ached in his chest. They sat silently, each wrapped in their own feelings and he discovered a compassion he had never felt for her before. He reached to cover her hand, again. Again, she withdrew at his touch.

"Please don't do that," she whispered.

"I only meant to comfort you."

"Please," she said, coolly. "Don't do that."

He cleared his throat, sipped his coffee. "How is Jenna this morning?"

"She's still sleeping."

"She said a nightmare woke her. Your disappearance really shook her up. That's why she called me."

"She must have found your business card taped to me computer."

"She was surprised I could see her."

"Being seen is very important to Jenna. It's the only way she knows she truly exists. Then again, it's the only time she gets hurt, being seen."

"Does Jenna have nightmares often?" Spencer asked.

"Lately, yes. Her father brought back some awful memories.

I've tried, but I can't keep them away." Jersey let go of a shaky sigh. "Every morning, I wake up feeling as if I've spent the night running for my life."

He started to put his hand on her shoulder, but she had rebuffed him twice. He reconsidered and let his hand fall. His newfound empathy for this woman/child surprised him. Spencer stood and went to refill his cup.

"More coffee, Jersey?" She held out her cup without turning. He brought the pot to the table, pouring her more. "How about some breakfast?" He suggested. "I'm starving."

"Thank you, no. But, please, help yourself. I've got the makings for just about anything."

Guilt panged as he moved about her kitchen. He felt like a Yankee soldier who had pillaged here before. "Looking in your cupboards, one can believe a child actually lives here."

"A child does live here," Jersey retorted. "In my house, Jenna gets everything she needs. Most of the time, she also gets what she wants."

Spencer busied his hands with eggs and cheese and salsa, while his mind busied itself with questions and doubts. He remembered Dr. Kaneally saying a child who suffered prolonged abuse split herself of from the bad person, in order to survive. Jenna had thought she was a bad girl, so she created Jersey? He looked at the woman sitting at the table, wearing the little girl's nightgown. He knew a person's heart could actually break, his had broken the day Belinda told him about Alison, and it might break again, now. The bottom line, he thought, was how the truth would play at her hearing, this afternoon. He buttered toast, topped cheese omelets with salsa and carried two plates to the table. Jersey pushed her plate away, but he slid it back to her.

"What are you trying to do, offend the chef?" He teased.

"Aren't your little police buddies expecting you?"

He bit into a piece of toast. "Not until this afternoon," he said, around his bite. "This morning, it is my distinct pleasure to serve you breakfast. If you don't want it, wake Jenna. Maybe, she's hungry."

"I don't do dog-and-pony shows." Her eyes snapped green fire. "If you're waiting for the crazy lady to flip out, you're wasting your morning."

"Thank you, it is my morning to waste." Frustration slugged him. "Besides, I love a good dose of self pity in the morning."

"How dare you! Why are you still here? I certainly didn't invite you."

"No, you're daughter invited me. I mean...." He set down his fork, caught her gaze. "Relax and eat, will you? I don't think you're crazy. I'm not expecting anything from you. Not even a thank you for staying with Jenna."

"What makes you think you know anything about me?"

"I told you, I know something about child abuse. Alison's therapist has helped her get over what happened to her. With the right help, you and Jenna could, too."

"Oh, my. You know something about child abuse," Jersey mocked, folding her arms across her chest. "Your little niece's therapist helped her get over what happened. Isn't that wonderful?" She hurled her cup across the room, shattering it against a cupboard. "I don't care what her therapist said. Your niece will live with her trauma every day of the rest of her life. She may learn to cope with it; she may learn to function in spite of it. But, she'll never get over it. Take my word on that."

"I do take you word on that, Jersey. I know how long you've functioned, in spite of it. But, you don't have to cope alone. You can't keep going by yourself."

"Yes, I can." She swept her hair out of her face and blew out her anger. "You don't know anything about me."

She forked up a mouthful of eggs, chewed methodically and swallowed. She looked as if he had stripped her of her skin, Spencer thought. He took his plate to the sink, stepping around the broken cup. He watched from the window as small brown sparrows swooped in the white sky. A breeze ruffled the leaves of a

Ficus tree against the glass. How could he prove to her that he only wanted to help?

"Jersey, can I ask you some really personal question?" He asked, finally. "I don't want to make you defensive, again. Please, help me understand."

"Ask whatever you like, that doesn't mean I'll answer."

"How long have you taken care of Jenna?"

"As long as I can remember." She got up, dampened a sponge at his side. She rested her hip against the counter, looking out the window with him. "I saw this TV show, when we were eight, about conjoining twins. Only we still called them Siamese twins, then. I figured if some twins could get stuck physically, maybe Jenna and I were twins who somehow never got separated at all. I grew up, but she never did."

"You have to know better than that, now." He turned to look at her. "When Daniel Miller molested Jenna, where were you?"

She threw the sponge into the sink and went to stare out the back door. She wrapped her arms around her, much as she had during their second interview, he thought.

"You kept him from her," he recalled her words. "That's what you said. Miller didn't molest Jenna when you could stop him." And, then he knew. "He molested you."

"I did what I had to." Jersey shrugged. "It was my job."

"Is that why you shot your father?"

"He wasn't my father, he was Jenna's father. I had to kill him, because she couldn't."

She laid her palm against a windowpane and gathered the flapping remnants of her dignity, folding the shreds around her bared soul. Spencer came up behind her and Jersey went very still, bracing herself for his touch. He raised his hands to her shoulders, heard her suck in air. She breathed out in short, rapid gasps, and he realized with a wrench of his heart that it was Jersey who thought she was the bad girl. Tears stung the backs of his eyes, and he dropped his hands.

"I won't touch you," he whispered. "I want to help you."

She threw back her head, taking a deep breath, and released a throaty laugh. She straightened her shoulders. "Thank you, so much," she disparaged. "My goodness, look at the time. I have an appointment with Judge Morgan, in an hour."

"Will you tell your attorney what you told me?"

Jersey turned, her features settling into a bland mask. "I haven't told you anything. It's only because of your fine detective skills that you know anything."

He cupped his face in his hands, exasperation glistening across his upper lip. "Then, will you tell him what I know?" He asked, through his hands. "Or, will I?"

"What you tell Cary Dodd, I cannot control," she said, stepping around him. "If you'll excuse me, I'm going to get out of this ridiculous nightgown. You look as if you could use a shower, yourself. Unfortunately, I only have one, and I never share."

She left him standing at the door.

Thursday, December 1

The small courtroom was paneled in grooved maple; acoustical tiles hung on the walls where windows should have been. A brass nameplate graced the lip of the high bench, announcing His Honor Judge Thornton Weimer, who had not as yet arrived. Jersey sat at a long, polished table beside Cary Dodd. ADA, Barbara Regon studied her notes at the other end of the table. They were here for the preliminary hearing, which was now a mere formality. Today, Jersey would learn the consequences of her actions on Halloween. Jenna clung to Jersey, pale and trembling.

"Don't be afraid, Honey Bunny," she whispered, keeping her voice between them.

"I'm scared they'll make you be in jail. Maybe that judge won't like it that I live here."

Jersey caressed her cheek. "That's why my friend Cary is here. He'll help the judge to understand everything."

A dozen seats made up the gallery. Suzanne Kirby and Spencer Phillips were the only spectators; no gate separated them. Phillips smiled at Jersey as she glanced past him. He had worn his blue jacket, today. He didn't appear nervous, she thought. Over the last four days, he had played a tennis match of conversations with Cary, Barbara Regon and Judge Weimer. He had vouched for Jenna's safety before Judge Morgan and somehow kept her out of a rubber room at the local psyche ward. Jersey didn't know why he had done any of it, but she was grateful he had.

Behind the judge's bench, the long hand on a large clock clicked straight up, nine a.m. A door in the wall opened and two bailiffs entered; Judge Weimer followed, with a court reporter on his heels. The judge was small man, his face etched and tanned, his head capped with thick, lead-gray curls. The five participants stood as he took his place on the bench. Jersey held on to Jenna. She took her seat with the others, butterflies dancing in her stomach. She smoothed away imaginary wrinkles in her navy wool skirt and tried to settle her nerves.

"Does the defense wish to waive the reading of rights and charges?" Judge Weimer asked.

Cary stood. "We're aware of the same, Your Honor. Defense so waives."

"Your Honor." Ms. Regon rose, now. "The People have accepted a plea from the defendant. Miss Masters had agreed to plead guilty to one count, negligent homicide."

"Yes, I've read the affidavits submitted by both parties." The judge eyeballed Jersey. Jenna shrank back. "Young woman, please stand." Jersey complied. "This plea is acceptable to you?"

"Yes, sir," she said, softly and sat, again.

"You have more, Ms. Regon?"

"Your Honor, we see no purpose served by incarcerating the defendant. However, my office stipulates she receive probation with the further understanding that she undergo psychiatric treatment for dissociative disorder. Dr. Suzanne Kirby, a licensed therapist of San Diego County, has agreed to treat Miss Masters."

"The court will accept your recommendations," he said, then pointed his gavel at Jersey. "Young lady, I sentence you to six years probation, on the understanding that you seek medical attention. In the event you discontinue treatment without completing your therapy, this court reserves the right to incarcerate you for the maximum time allowed by law. Do you understand this?"

She swallowed and nodded. "Yes."

"This matter is adjourned." Judge Weimer banged his gavel.

"Is it over, Jersey?" Jenna whispered, tremulously.

"In a way, it's just beginning," she said. She allowed the child to slip from her lap, but she kept a firm hold on her.

"You don't have to be in jail, right, Jersey?"

"No, I don't. Remember I told you we might have to talk to Ms. Kirby, though? The judge thinks that's a good idea."

"I will like that, too. She makes me good cocoa."

Jersey smiled. "Some things are going to change for us, I think."

"But, you won't go away, again, will you Jersey?"

"I certainly don't intend to." She stroked Jenna's hair.

Everyone stood as the judge and his entourage left the room. Jersey turned to her attorney, while Jenna watched him from behind. Jersey extended her hand; Cary took it in both of his.

"Now, you can thank me," he said, smiling.

"I do, very much. Call me and I'll design your next advertising layout free of charge."

"That, however, will not affect my bill."

"Understood." Jersey said, and laughed.

Spencer stepped to her side. "Congratulations, Miss Masters," he said. "I'm very glad for the way things turned out."

"Thank you, so am I." She gave him a genuine smile, a first.

Cary stepped away to speak to Barbara Regon and Spencer stepped closer. Caution narrowed her eyes, instinctively.

"This isn't the right place to say this," he said. "But, I don't know if I'll have another chance. I'd like to get to know you better, on a personal level."

"Yeah, I want to, Jersey." Jenna tugged at her. "He's nice to me."

"I don't know," she said, addressing them both. "I don't do personal, very well."

"I've grown very fond of Jenna, during this case, and... I mean—"

Jersey quirked an eyebrow at him. "What would your friends think of you dating a six-year-old?"

"That's not what I meant." Spencer flushed, a familiar ire settling in his gut. "You are a most exasperating woman."

"Thank you." She issued a simpering smile. "I do try."

His coat pocket rang. "Excuse me."

He walked to the back of the courtroom, taking his phone from the pocket of his blue sport coat. Suzanne Kirby still waited at her seat. Jersey approached her now, feeling like a specimen in a jar. Very soon, this woman would know everything about her, and Jersey didn't like the idea, at all. Suzanne smiled and held out her hand. Jenna took it.

"So, we'll be spending the next six years together," Jersey said, smiling wryly. "How much did you want to know about me?"

"As I explained to you yesterday, Jersey, we're making a commitment to each other. I agree to be available to you, when you need me. In return, you agree to show up and to be as honest as you can."

"I don't want to lose Jenna," she blurted.

Suzanne brushed her fingertips down Jersey's arm. "It isn't about losing either one of you. It's about finding each other, again. Your father stole something very precious from you. I'm going to help you get her back."

"You ladies ready to go?" Cary asked, jauntily swinging his briefcase.

Spencer joined them now. Jersey looked from Cary to Suzanne to him. "We're going to celebrate over brunch," she said. "You're welcome to join us, if you like."

"Thanks, but I can't. My case load has suffered greatly, the last couple of months."

Jersey felt an unfamiliar twinge. Was it disappointment? She shrugged it away; it wasn't important. "Don't let us keep you, then, Detective." She looked to Cary and Suzanne. "We're ready," she said.

Christmas Eve, December 24

"Is it time to turn on our Christmas lights, yet, Jersey?" Jenna asked, and sipped her cocoa.

"Not yet, Honey Bunny, but soon. By the time we finish decorating our tree, it should be dark enough."

Jersey settled the last strand of lights in the fir branches and knelt to plug them in. Tiny white lights sprang to life, twinkling and chasing each other. The pungent aroma of the six-foot Blue Spruce mingled with the rich sweetness of raspberry truffle cocoa. She and Jenna had cut their own tree from a lot in El Cajon, right after breakfast. Jersey smiled, recalling the fun they had tromping through row after row of bright green firs, breathing the pine scent with the crisp winter air. Jenna had loved playing hide-and-seek, until they found just the right tree. They were both still wearing the Christmas sweaters she had bought for the outing. Jersey teamed hers with denim-colored leggings and pinned her hair back with silver combs.

"We'll leave the lights on while we decorate, okay?"

Jersey laid out boxes of ornaments on the sofa, while Jenna munched a gingerbread man. Andy Williams sang, "it's the most wonderful time of the year," from the stereo and Jersey hummed along. It was a most wonderful time, she thought. A fire snapped and popped in the fireplace; her collection of brass and raffia angels was on the mantel, framed with a garland of holly and white lights. Stockings for Jenna and Jersey hung at each corner of the mantel. A plate of cookies and a pot of hot chocolate sat on the coffee table. A centerpiece of candles glowed on the dining room table; dozens of silver glass balls were suspended in the windows on red satin ribbons; Bedford Falls was set up on her office credenza. Jenna chose a hand-carved wooden burro and carried it to the tree. Jersey caught a look of worry on her sweet face.

"What's wrong, Honey Bunny?"

"I am thinkin', maybe I'm not getting my presents now." She slid the ornament over a bough, with no joy.

"Oh, Jenna. Why would you think that?"

Her chin quivered. "Maybe, Santa Claus won't come at my house. Maybe, he's thinkin' I'm a bad girl, now."

"You're not a bad girl, Jenna. Santa Claus knows that." Jersey wrapped the child in her arms. "Suzanne told you, what your daddy did was not your fault. He was bad, not you. Don't you believe her?"

Jenna nodded, but she still looked worried.

"You don't have to worry," Jersey said, smiling. "Santa Claus will come just like always, I promise."

In fact, Jenna's presents were already wrapped and hidden in her study closet. Tomorrow morning, Jenna would wake to find a brand new doll baby in a wicker buggy from Santa, and an easel and paints from her. Gifts from Jersey's family had already arrived and she planned to put them out, once the tree was decorated. She had mailed off presents for her family weeks ago. She didn't go home for Christmas. She believed Christmas was for children, and she couldn't let Jenna celebrate unless they were here.

Jersey stood back, watching Jenna hang raffia stars and straw baskets on the tree. Where would they be next year, she wondered? They had seen Suzanne twice a week for the last three weeks. Things progressed slowly, as the three grew comfortable with each other. Although Suzanne had a working knowledge of Jenna's abuse, Jersey felt uneasy having the truth come out. She wanted to trust Suzanne not to use the information to harm them, but she didn't trust Suzanne.

Maybe I don't have the mechanisms for trust, Jersey thought. Jenna trusted the woman, implicitly. She could spend an entire session chattering away about every memory and detail. Jersey often had to hold the child back. Her memories were pretty gruesome, after all. And, Jersey wanted to monitor how much to tell and how soon, just in case.

Jenna dangled tiny sombreros and painted burros in the tree, her eyes glowing happily, now. Through the front window, Jersey saw her neighbors stringing lights across the eaves of their homes. The tree always looked beautiful in the front window, she thought. Andy Williams started singing "Jingle Bells" and Jenna joined him. Jersey chuckled as the little girl tried, but didn't quite match, the swing tempo. Would this be their last Christmas together, she wondered? Would Jenna outgrow her by next year? Would the child end up taking back the life her father robbed of her?

"Maybe, I'm the one who'll end up alone," she murmured, her heart aching.

"Hmm?" Jenna said.

"Nothing, Honey Bunny." She smiled. "Are you having a good time?"

"Mm hmm!"

Neither of them would go, Jersey decided, shaking her head. She would never allow that to happen. Jenna would die without her, and Jenna's mental health would not come at her own demise. Suzanne had assured her neither would be lost in the healing process. Rather, she said they would come together, eventually leaving a whole, functioning personality. Whatever that was, she mused. Such a concept was too foreign. She and Jenna were two people and always had been. How could they ever become one?

"Is it dark enough, yet, now, Jersey?" Jenna began to dance with anticipation.

"Sure it is," she said, with a chuckle. "Let's turn on the outside lights."

The two raced through the foyer and out the front door, Jenna squealing, madly. Jersey hurried around the corner where an extension cord hung from the roof and plugged it into the outlet beside the chimney, bringing the house to life. Jenna clapped her hands. Fairy lights twinkled in the crepe myrtle and the cinnamon ferns. Strands of tiny lights framed the house. Mr. and Mrs. Claus exchanged a Christmas kiss on the front porch. Jenna and Jersey stood on the lawn, admiring the beautiful scene.

Cars slowed as they drove passed. Others in the neighborhood also displayed their holiday spirit as night tamped out the sun. A familiar brown sedan pulled into her driveway. Jersey turned, as Detective Phillips stepped out of his car. Though he was driving the company car, he wore jeans and a black sweater. He lifted out a small cardboard box tied with a big green bow, and carried it toward her.

"No wonder your neighbors are so impressed with your light display," he said, admiring the firefly points of light.

"Thanks, but I can't take all the credit. I hire a couple of college students every year, to help me."

"This is for Jenna," he said, holding out the box. "She'll need to open it right away. No dog-and-pony shows," he added quickly. "I just wanted her to have it."

Jersey allowed the child to accept it. Jenna crouched in the grass and pulled off the ribbon, tossing it away. As she lifted the lid, a small gray puff of fur scrambled out.

"Oh, boy!" Jenna squealed. " 's a kitty! 's a kitty!"

"He's probably about ten weeks old," Spencer said. "I rescued him from the Dumpster at my apartment building. He's had some shots, but he'll need to be neutered. I'll take care of that, too, when it's time."

Jersey stood and gave him a wry smile. "I'm sold, Detective."

"Could you try calling me Spencer?"

"I suppose I could try. If I really have to." Jersey smirked. She scooped up the little cat and let Jenna hold it.

"I like your sweater, very festive." Spencer smiled. "So, have you two done any Christmas caroling? Spread any holiday cheer?"

"I took Jenna to the living nativity at Balboa Park, and she got a phone call from Santa. She can't exactly visit him at the local mall."

"I suppose not," he said, watching the little girl nuzzle the kitten. He had wanted to make Jenna smile, and had succeeded. It felt good - right. "What will she name it?"

"She's calling him Dusty."

He stepped closer, his mouth suddenly dry. "We never finished our conversation at the courthouse." She looked down at Jenna, murmuring to her kitten. "More precisely, you never gave me an answer about seeing each other, personally."

"I can't begin to think about that," Jersey said, her heart thudding against her ribs. "We - Jenna and I - we have too many questions to answer. I'm not sure where we'll be, once we do."

"I understand." He stared at his shoes. "I'm going to be thirty-seven, in a few weeks. For most of my adult life, my sister's family has been my family. Lately, I'm realizing how tired I am of being alone. Do you know what I mean?"

"I do." She met his eyes that shined with appeal.

"I'm not asking you to elope, or to make any commitment you're not capable of. I'm asking you to think of me as your friend. And, to let me be a part of whatever comes next for you."

"Say yes, Jersey," Jenna pleaded. "Say yes, 'kay?"

"I'm not good at being friends, either. I've never done it before. And, I warn you, you may never be rid of Jenna, once she gets attached."

"Fair enough," he said, with a smile.

The kitten flipped cartwheels across the lawn and Jenna giggled. They stood, watching as it pounced on shifting grass blades and darted after the loose ribbon.

"Spencer, we baked gingerbread men, yesterday," Jersey said. "Would you like to have one, with a cup of coffee?"

His smile appreciated the gesture. "I'm due at my sister's, but I'll give her a call. Homemade cookies sound good."